T0196068

NATHANIEL

TRIPP DAVIS

WESTBOW
PRESS®
A DIVISION OF THOMAS NELSON
& ZONDERVAN

WestBow Press books may be ordered through booksellers or by contacting:

WestBow Press
A Division of Thomas Nelson & Zondervan
1663 Liberty Drive
Bloomington, IN 47403
www.westbowpress.com
1 (866) 928-1240

ISBN: 978-1-9736-0551-5 (sc)
ISBN: 978-1-9736-0552-2 (hc)
ISBN: 978-1-9736-0550-8 (e)

Library of Congress Control Number: 2017914878

Print information available on the last page.

WestBow Press rev. date: 10/17/2017

To my wife Jennifer, the adventure we have
lived couldn't have been imagined when we met.
From snowy mountains to lunches in towers, I couldn't
have dreamed living this life with anyone but you.

Mary went ahead anyway, telling the servants,
"Whatever he tells you, do it."
—John 2:5

PROLOGUE

"Azeem, Azeem! Come quickly, Azeem!"

"Coming, my lord," Azeem cried as he came running into the room, out of breath. He looked around frantically and found his master standing at the rail on the balcony staring at the night sky.

"Azeem!"

"I'm here, my lord. What's troubling you?"

"Troubling me? Troubling me?" Balthazar turned around quickly and embraced his servant, letting out a deep belly laugh as he hugged his servant and picked him up off the ground and spun in a circle. "Troubling me? You wonderful servant! You wonderful friend!"

Balthazar put him down and pulled him closer to the rail so quickly that Azeem feared he might fall over. Balthazar pointed to the starry heavens and said, "Do you see that? Azeem, do you see that?"

Azeem looked up and saw a magnificent star—a star as he had never seen before. It was so beautiful, and he was quite sure he would have remembered this star, yet he had never seen it before.

"Master, it is wonderful," Azeem muttered as he stared in amazement. Both men stared for several minutes, marveling at its splendor and beauty. It was unlike anything they had seen before.

Balthazar urgently spoke in a whisper. "Azeem."

"Yes, my lord?" Azeem responded quietly as they both stood still, mesmerized by the spectacle in the sky.

Balthazar turned toward Azeem and grabbed his shoulders, looking at him with an intensity Azeem had only seen before a battle. With the excitement fading from his voice, he spoke with a sense of urgency, with the authority of a king. "I need you to do something for me—something more important than anything you have ever done before."

"Of course, my lord, anything. You need only to say the word," Azeem responded respectfully.

"By now, Gaspar and Melchior have seen the star. I need you to go to the stables and get our fastest steed and ride like the wind. Ride all night and bring them both. Repeat to them exactly what I tell you and nothing else. Do you understand?"

"Of course, master," Azeem said with a puzzled look on his face.

"Tell them these words from the holy text: 'A star will come out of Jacob; a scepter will rise out of Israel' [Numbers 24:17 NIV]. They will understand these words and will gather their things for the journey. Tell them to bring gifts for a king. Tell them to bring some frankincense and gold." Balthazar's voice rose as Azeem headed across the massive palace courtyard toward a large door leading into the garden and stables.

"Go now quickly, for there is a great distance to travel. When you return with them, the three of us will begin our journey. Hurry—go quickly, for something wonderful has happened tonight!"

"Yes, master!" Azeem shouted as he ran from the room.

Balthazar smiled as he watched Azeem run across the courtyard toward the stables, the cool breeze blowing away the dust trail that followed him. He looked back toward the heavens and was once again filled with amazement, and for a moment, he felt like a child again.

"God had returned to his people. A king is born this very night. A king that will save the world."

Chapter 1

Slowly, Nathaniel opened his eyes and reached over for Sera, knowing she wasn't there. The smells of roasting fish and hot bread floating in the air—combined with the welcome sound of a crackling fire through the house—confirmed that she had gotten up already.

He rolled over, eyes still closed, feeling for the warmth from where she had slept and didn't find it. It was winter in Nazareth, and the cold seeping through the shutters had claimed that spot. He was still in that hazy state where yawns and stretches feel so good, so he rolled over and pulled the blanket under his chin. Slowly, he opened his eyes and leaned up on one elbow until he found the perfect view he was looking for. There she was. Just past the door between two pillars, Nathaniel could see his wife. She was kneading fresh dough, and the fire she had built gave her face a warm glow. Deep in thought, she had a familiar smile, almost as if she was looking at their friend in person.

Nathaniel looked over at the small table and half smiled, seeing the pair of doves he had carved for them on their wedding day. It had been three months this very day since their friend was killed. Even as he marveled at the beauty of his wife and felt so fortunate to have her, he couldn't deny the pain he felt inside and the yearning to see his friend again face-to-face.

"Nathaniel." Sera's voice startled him as he thought about the amazing things that had transpired and regretted that he didn't realize sooner who his friend actually was.

"I know you're awake, and I know you're staring at me again," she said with a smile and a glance.

Nathaniel quickly wiped the tears from his eyes and rolled over, stretching, and said, "I can't help myself; you look like a spring flower."

"You're a silly man." She felt embarrassed even though she loved the admiration her husband showed her. Sera had green piercing eyes and dark skin, roughened slightly by the dry wind that blew through Nazareth and the hot Middle Eastern sun. Even with that, she was absolutely beautiful. Many of Nathaniel's friends had had ideas of marrying her, but he was the one who got her father's approval.

"You know, there's a man standing by the gate, and he's been there all morning. Why don't you come and eat, and then you can see what he wants."

Nathaniel had come up behind her and put his hands around her waist, and then, he whispered in her ear, "Maybe he wants something fixed or a whole house full of furniture." Then he kissed her on the ear.

"Stop that," she said quietly as she leaned back into his embrace. He spun her around and looked deeply into her eyes and smiled.

"Number one, breakfast is ready," she said, and quickly gave him a playful kiss on the cheek. "Number two, you have a customer outside, and you need to eat the breakfast that I have prepared for you." She kissed him on his other cheek as she ducked out of his embrace, laughing as she hurried to set the table.

Nathaniel smiled, watching her run toward the window to set the table that he had made. It wasn't his best work, but Sera loved it because it was the first thing he made in his carpentry shop after they were married.

His smile slowly began to fade when he opened the shutters and saw the shrouded figure standing at the gate. Nathaniel could clearly see scars on the man's partially covered face as he looked up toward the morning sun with his eyes closed. He simply stood there with one hand slightly raised, either enjoying the heat from the morning sun or praying. At that moment, the stranger slowly turned toward Nathaniel and smiled. His eyes were almost gold, like those of a tiger, which gave him a distinguished look with his dark skin and well-trimmed gray beard. Nathaniel waved slightly and mouthed the words "I'll be right out."

The stranger acknowledged this with a nod, the pleasant expression never leaving his face.

Nathaniel remained at the window, mesmerized by the thought that the man seemed familiar in some way. He thought maybe it was the eyes or the smile. He wasn't sure. But there was something.

"Sera," Nathaniel mumbled, "would you ... um, set another—"

"I already have, my love," she said with a smile, while busying herself with setting an extra plate for the stranger. "Now go," she prodded as she got behind him and pushed him toward the front door.

Nathaniel grabbed her and kissed her. "Thank you," he said, anxiously making his way out into the vast courtyard. Walking toward the gate, he pulled his tunic over his head as he approached the stranger.

Nathaniel had inherited their home from his father, who was a successful businessman and a great teacher when it came to business and life in general. Nathaniel inherited his skill for business and succeeded at everything he set out to. Although he had a remarkable gift for business for an uneducated man, his first love was working with wood. Every piece was unique, with different textures and colors, and as good as Nathaniel was at trading livestock and goods, he had unmatched carpentry skills.

"Herut, come quickly. We have a guest." Nathaniel spoke loudly to one of his hired servants as he approached the stranger.

"Good morning," Nathaniel said as he ushered the man into the stone courtyard. "Welcome, welcome. Please ... please come in." Nathaniel stumbled over his words, caught off guard by the severity of the scars on the man's hands, face, and neck. He had seen thieves and murderers beaten by the Romans, but this man obviously had wealth, judging by the fine linen garments that he wore. What could have possibly caused such a horrible thing to happen? Nathaniel suddenly became aware that he was staring and stammered out a quick apology. "I'm sorry, I didn't mean—"

"It's all right, Nathaniel. You are Nathaniel?" the man asked as he slowly walked into the open courtyard toward the animals in the stalls. He reached toward a donkey as Nathaniel said, "Yes, I am. Be careful, he—" and that's all he could get out when trying to warn the man that the animal bit people. Awestruck, Nathaniel stood there as the animal bowed his head in submission and responded calmly to the stranger's touch.

"My name is Simon. It's good to meet you. There, there," he said to the donkey, continuing to rub his head.

Nathaniel watched Simon with the beast. He was gentle, yet he had an air of authority. He had seen authority his whole life, dealing with the Romans and wealthy merchants, but had only seen this kind gentleness in one other man.

At that moment, Herut, Nathaniel's servant, came running in out of breath with a cup of water in his hand. He was covered from head to toe in mud and stood with his head bowed, trying to catch his breath. Nathaniel met Herut when he took a job in Bethlehem. He had become a skilled carpenter and was like a son to him and Sera.

"I'm ... sorry ... master." Herut gasped as he breathed heavily between his words.

"Herut, what happened?" Nathaniel spoke with concern.

"One of the new lambs, master ... One of them got out and thought to make his escape, but I caught him in the neighbor's garden." Herut looked up with a huge smile, proud of his accomplishment. The mud covering most of his face contrasted with his unusually white teeth, making him quite a sight to see.

Nathaniel glanced at Simon and handed him the cup of water that Herut held. Simon thanked him as he continued to watch the scenario unfold. Nathaniel's response to his servant would go a long way in showing Simon what kind of man he was dealing with. Nathaniel surveyed the situation and turned and winked at Simon.

"Herut!" Nathaniel said sternly. "Today, I want you to plant a new garden."

"Yes, master, whatever you wish," Herut responded, surprised by the sternness in his master's voice. Herut had his head bowed and did not see that both Simon and Nathaniel were smiling.

"And when you do, please use all the soil you have brought from the neighbor's garden." Nathaniel and Simon began to laugh, and Herut looked up with the same smile and began to laugh with them.

"Good job, Herut. Now, go clean up yourself, quickly," Nathaniel said with a smile.

"Yes, master," Herut responded as he ran across the courtyard, still smiling, relieved that he hadn't embarrassed his master.

"Please forgive me, Simon. I have kept you much too long. Please, let's go to the shop. I have several pieces to show you," Nathaniel said as he began to usher Simon across the courtyard.

Simon politely followed and said, "Nathaniel, I'm the one who needs to apologize." They both entered the shop together. Simon began to look at the furniture pieces. "I actually came to talk to you about a man who helped me once when I was in a very dark place in my life."

Nathaniel listened. He pulled cloth covers away from the windows to allow the bright morning sun to illuminate the shop. He tied the covers to the top of the windows with leather straps and motioned Simon over to a large table in the middle of the room near the fireplace.

"Please, sit down. Let me light a fire," Nathaniel said. He stacked a few logs onto some wood shavings and lit them.

Simon asked, "So you made all of this?" He waved his arm across the room with a smile.

"I did, with the help of Herut. He is more of a son than a hired servant, and a very gifted carpenter."

"As is his master," Simon remarked as he rubbed his hand over the intricate carving on the corner of the table.

"Thank you, Simon," Nathaniel said as he fanned the growing flames in the fireplace.

"Good morning," Sera announced when she knocked on the wooden door and ushered Herut into the shop.

Herut had cleaned himself up, and he carried a large covered tray, which he set in the middle of the table. He looked at both Simon and his master and bowed as he moved backward out of the shop.

Nathaniel smiled as he looked at his wife. "Simon, this is my wife, Sera."

Simon, smiling back, said, "Good morning, Sera. It is a pleasure to meet you."

"Good morning. I have brought you some breakfast," Sera said cheerfully. She quickly set out plates with napkins, figs, dates, hot bread, fish, and a bowl of olive oil. As she poured two cups of wine, she stopped midpour and looked at Simon. It was as if time stood still. "You knew him. You knew him, didn't you?" she asked when she noticed the scars on his face.

The awkwardness of the moment paralyzed Nathaniel, and he wasn't sure what had just happened. Sera began to apologize as Simon stood up and walked toward the door. "I'm sorry. I didn't mean …" she stammered.

Simon changed directions and walked to the windows to close the shutters and pull down the covers. "Please," he said. He paused and walked back to the fire. He just stood and stared at it, warming his hands for what seemed like an eternity. "Please forgive me. The cold and these old bones are at odds with each other." Simon smiled and slowly made his way back around the table. He motioned for Sera to sit between him and Nathaniel.

"Please join us," Simon pleaded to Sera. He looked at her with a painful smile and said, "Yes, I did … I did know him."

At this point, Nathaniel was completely lost. He felt fairly certain Sera and Simon didn't know each other. Maybe they had met in the market or had had business in the past. Nathaniel couldn't take it and said, "How …"

Simon raised a hand and said, "Please let me explain."

No one touched the food. Nathaniel and Sera intently watched Simon. A reflection of the fire danced off Simon's piercing eyes as he started to speak.

"It all began so simply. A caravan of Midianite traders came across my path one day." Simon turned toward them. "All I wanted was to buy some spices and fabric for my wife. I had dealt with them before, and they knew me. I had traded with them many times."

Simon reached for a cup of wine and continued. "This time, they had come from Egypt and had acquired some statues of gods. They were beautifully handpainted, and one in particular caught my attention. The traders told me his name was Bisu and that he brought good fortune and luck. He was very ornate, and I thought he would look good at the entrance in my home. They wrapped a few of them up, and I gave my wife a few smaller ones to set around our home. I took the statue of Bisu. He was as high as my waist. I set him on a stone table so I could jokingly look him in the eye when I asked him for good luck." But Simon wasn't laughing or even smiling. He had a look of regret and pain on his face.

"It was just a trinket to me or a good-luck symbol. I never thought twice about it, really," Simon continued. "I began to joke around the house, coming in and going out. I would raise my arms and say, 'Come to me, Bisu. Bring me all you have.' It was a joke. Everyone laughed and had a good time with it all. However, all my businesses started to increase, and somehow, I began to feel it was connected to Bisu, so I would speak with him as I came and went. Looking back, it was all so strange. I began to focus on profit more, and my business became even more profitable. As absurd as it sounds, I felt as if Bisu was talking to me and showing me how to make more money. He would tell me secrets, and I began to lose focus on the fact that I was talking to a statue. But it was exciting and … intoxicating."

Simon paused as he searched for the words. From his gaze and expression, Nathaniel and Sera could tell he was in a different time and place. "So much so I began to reason with him and have serious conversations. At that point, it no longer had anything to do with the statue. It just started that way." Simon looked at them both as he raised his hands and felt the scars on his face. "However, it didn't stay that way," Simon said with a heavy look of guilt. "I'm so ashamed … my family and everything I have put them through. I can't—"

"It's okay," Sera said in a comforting voice.

"Please, tell us what happened," Nathaniel added.

"At that point, I realized I was dealing with something real—something or someone outside of me, so to speak. I was scared, and yet the allure was so thrilling I couldn't help it. There was actually something around me, or with me, at that point, following me and talking to me. He was saying he was my friend and would help me do things that no one had done before. Soon, I felt invincible, until one day … one day, Bisu told me everything would be easier and that he could communicate with me better from the inside. I didn't understand, but he had only helped me up to that point, and I was keeping this from my family and those who worked under me. He said that I didn't have to even talk out loud—that he could read my thoughts from the inside. What did I have to lose? As it turned out, a great deal."

Simon stood up and began to walk toward the window. "Forgive me; I need some air." He cracked open the shutter just enough to allow crisp, cool air to rush in, carrying the sweet smell of freshly falling rain. He stood there for a moment with his eyes closed, taking in the aroma and fresh air, seemingly lost in his thoughts.

"Simon," Nathaniel said after a few moments, "please come finish your story."

"Yes, of course," Simon responded and then walked back to the table and sat down. "Things began to unravel from that point on," Simon continued. "I began to forget things. I lost track of time, only to be accused of stealing something or cursing at someone. I couldn't remember any of it. I began to have vile thoughts about abusing my children. My wife woke me up one night and said I was choking her. My health began to deteriorate. I began to drink strong drink day and night just to sleep. Eventually, even that didn't help. My friends and family said I looked horrible. My children wouldn't come near me. Four of my sons had to pull me off a man in the street. They said I was screaming at him in another language and trying to kill him because I didn't like the way he looked at me when we passed each other. I'll never forget the looks of fear and confusion in their eyes as I came back to myself. It haunts me to this day.

"By that time, I was very afraid, and I could feel Bisu begin to take over. I remember feeling hatred, horrible anger as I've never felt. But it wasn't me. It was Bisu. He would start on me the same every time. I always felt fear, but when he came ... when he came ..." Simon tried to hold back his emotions, but tears fell from his eyes, reflecting the firelight in the darkened room.

"When he came, a piercing cold would shoot through me like a hundred arrows through my body. A foul stench would choke me and burn my eyes. He would squeeze me until I thought my bones would break. Suddenly, it would get darker and darker, and I could only see red, like looking through your own blood, and the fear ... the fear was ...," Simon just sat staring at the fire. His face had grown pale, and the tears had stopped falling. His eyes were glazed and empty. An eerie silence was interrupted by the crackling of the fire.

Simon jumped and Sera screamed as Nathaniel also jumped back. The three of them froze, staring at one another. They shyly grinned as they realized that all the commotion started when Nathaniel had reached behind Sera and had placed his hand on Simon's back to comfort him. The three sat for a moment, laughing as a griping, dark intensity lifted from the room.

Simon sat back in his chair. He wiped his face with a napkin from the table and neatly folded it, running his hands over the creases several times as he continued his story. "This nightmare continued until I could no longer control myself at all," he said, glancing at them both. "I would eat foul things and then vomit. Often, I would be thrown to the other side of the room or up onto the ceiling only to come crashing down to the floor. My poor wife and children were so terrified that my sons and friends chained me up outside the city. This happened several times. I would break the chains and wake up with cuts and bruises all over my body. This went on for months.

"I lived in complete fear and confusion and a darkness that is indescribable. I even tried to take my own life several times, but Bisu wouldn't let me. Instead of letting me kill myself, he tried to make me kill others. I lost all hope. Every day was horrific torture. Rage and fury mixed with my horrible, deviant thoughts, and my actions were out of my control, until one morning, he came."

Simon paused and began to smile. Staring back into the fire, he reached with one hand toward the warmth as he shivered. "All I can remember is that I stood in pain by a rock. I was bloody and cut up from the night before. Suddenly, I felt fear as I had never felt before, but it wasn't me who was afraid. It was Bisu. At that moment, a chorus of horrific screaming inside me was so painful that I dropped to the ground in agony. At that moment, I realized Bisu wasn't one but many. They all hissed like snakes and screamed together at once. 'No!' they screamed. 'No, he's coming! He's coming, no!' Over and over, they chanted. I could feel their terror.

"As I fought for control, I strained with everything within me to look toward the sea. I gasped for air and trembled as I felt every one of them screaming through me. I couldn't really make it out. It was so bright, like looking into the sun. It hurt so bad to look. It looked like … like a massive bright light walking toward me in the shape of a man, and the closer he got to me, the more they screamed. I convulsed with pain and began to vomit. Bisu took control and stood me up with a thrust. I could feel his fear. The rest of the demons trembled and tried to find someplace to hide inside of me.

"As this man approached, my body convulsed in pain as Bisu flung me back to the ground. I was forced to slide forward like a child's toy on a string being pulled through the sand. I felt what I thought was a spear thrust through my skull. I grabbed my head in pain as thousands of voices began to scream and curse in rebellion. Now, Bisu was afraid. They all were afraid—very afraid. I could see his outline on and off through waves of nausea as he approached, but I couldn't see his face," Simon said in frustration.

"The man stood over me. Somehow, I knew he was there to help, but I struggled to breathe. I felt like I was drowning," Simon said with a look of confusion. "I began to make out his features the closer he got. His eyes were gentle and peaceful yet had a strength that I can't describe, and there was a brilliant radiance all around him, like looking at sunlight through water. Then he spoke."

Simon paused and looked at both Nathaniel and Sera with a look of amazement. "He spoke to Bisu in a voice of authority that I had never heard before, or since. He didn't shout. There was such a peaceful intensity and power in his voice that it brought me the one thing I desperately needed: hope. He spoke to them all, and it made them scream as if daggers were being pushed into each one's body. They started begging him to let them stay. They hated him and feared him. They chanted, 'Son of God, Son of God,' and they begged him not to torment them. I don't know if he could hear them like I could, but it sounded like thousands of babies crying and dogs growling and whimpering all at the same time. I was paralyzed with fear and on the brink of losing my mind when he raised his hand and said, 'Be quiet.'

"As violently as it all started, everything suddenly stopped. The screams, the sounds, everything—it all stopped. They trembled, and they began whispering a thousand whispers back and forth like a pit of vipers. They were so scared, whirring through my body. I could feel their anticipation of something—something he would do to them. Then he spoke again, and he didn't speak to me. He asked Bisu, 'What is your name?' I felt an arrogant unity respond in many voices. 'I am Legion, for we are many.' Yet, behind the vulgar arrogance, there was fear. Bisu tried to hide a desperate and confused fear. Then a curious thing happened. Bisu began to beg and bargain with this man, this stranger, this savior!" Simon exclaimed with exuberance.

"'Please don't send us into the dry places! You're merciful, merciful, merciful!' Bisu begged in agony and screamed in a thousand voices, 'The pigs, the pigs ... let us go into the *pigs*!' They all began to whisper back and forth in frenzied chaos. The chorus grew louder and louder, saying, 'The pigs, the pigs ... let us go into the *pigs*!' over and over, again and again. I couldn't take it!" Simon almost shouted and grabbed his head, reliving the very moment.

"Simon, it's okay." Sera spoke with a gentle voice while looking over at Nathaniel as he nodded in approval. Simon had backed his chair away from the table. He dropped his hands into his lap in relief as his breathing returned to normal. He wiped sweat from his brow. Nathaniel and Sera both had turned their chairs toward Simon's and were leaning in, eagerly awaiting the continuation of his story, although they both knew this stranger was their friend and they knew how this story would end.

Simon sat back in his chair. Now, he was relaxed and had a look of serenity. He reflected and began the last of his story. But when he looked at Nathaniel and Sera, he hesitated. "He ended the ordeal with one word: *go*. He simply said, 'Go.'" Simon looked at them both with a confused look. "I still don't understand; after all I had been through—weeks and weeks of begging and pleading with Bisu to leave me—and he just says, 'Go'?" Simon half smiled as he shook his head in disbelief.

"And Bisu left. They all left. It was like a fierce wind blew through the inside of me, and they had no choice but to leave. It felt like I was torn open and instantly closed up when they tried to grab hold of my insides. I fell limp on the ground, and they rushed out and headed toward a herd of pigs. You know, I felt the agony of the squealing pigs as they ran into the sea and drowned themselves." Simon shook his head in disgust.

"I slowly opened my eyes, and there he was, sitting on the ground embracing me. And all my emotions emptied there as I cried and held on to him like life itself. 'There now, Simon, it's all right now. They are gone and won't return,' he said to me and smiled. He was … I mean, it was all …" Simon hesitated. "The contrast of the fear and agony, being suddenly gone and this … this love that I didn't realize existed. I … I can't explain." Simon struggled to get the words out and was overwhelmed with emotion. "He kept telling me that he loved me and everything was going to be all right."

Simon raised his hands to his face, cried freely for a moment, and then began to collect himself. "It's all right, my brother. It's all right." Nathaniel comforted him. Sera wiped her own tears from her eyes.

After a moment, Simon clasped his hands under his chin and continued. "One of his followers brought out a basket of fish and some bread. Words cannot describe how good that simple meal was." Simon chuckled and Nathaniel smiled as heaviness lifted from the room.

"We all sat and ate and talked for a while until a large group of men from my village approached us with sticks and rocks. It seems that the pig herders saw the whole thing and went and told the villagers what had happened. They were frightened and angry at the loss of their herd, but they couldn't come right out and say this man had killed the pigs. Many of them were my neighbors and knew I would make it right after they saw I was in my right mind," Simon said with a smile that had a hint of regret.

"They did say, however, that this stranger was not welcome and had to go. I looked over at him, and he just smiled and nodded to the men with him and headed back toward his boat. I chased after him and begged him to let me go with him, but he told me to go home, that my family would welcome me, and to tell everyone what a glorious thing God had done for me that day. And he was gone."

Simon stood up, stretched, and began to straighten things nervously, almost embarrassed by his emotions and the possibility that Nathaniel and Sera thought he was crazy. "I know this all sounds unusual, but a man named Paul told me to come see you. He said you would tell me more about him. His name was—"

"Jesus," Nathaniel interrupted with a confident smile. "His name was Jesus, and yes, I knew him well." His smile grew bigger, along with Sera's. "He was my friend, and it's going to take longer than breakfast to tell you his story. Can you stay for a few days, Simon?" Nathaniel asked while moving the food to a smaller table a little closer to the fire.

Sera tied up the leather shades inside the shutters to bring in more of the midday light. "There, that's better," she said. She arranged two chairs with beautifully embroidered red cushions that she had made. "Sit here; these will be more comfortable. Please."

She motioned for Simon to try them out. She waited to see

his smile of approval, which he quickly gave, easing back and stretching. And he said, "Wonderful. Thank you."

Sera arranged the food and an oil lamp on the table. Then she paused and smiled. "Simon, you know, he used to sit in that very chair when he would come to visit." Simon smiled as he looked down and rubbed the arms of the chair, trying to imagine what that was like. Nathaniel paused, remembering his friend's smile, and remembering sitting across from him in that chair. And for the first time in several months, he felt the pain of the ordeal beginning to subside.

"Well, my friend," Nathaniel said while leaning over to add wood to the fire, "your timing is perfect. Sera and I just spent time with Mary, Jesus's mother. There was so much I didn't know. And as remarkable as your story is, you will never be the same when I tell you who he really was."

CHAPTER 2

Josiah walked out of his workshop and headed across the courtyard, two large chairs in tow. He looked up at the sky and closed his eyes, inhaling deeply, smelling fragrant spring flowers in the afternoon breeze. He just stood there as the sun warmed his face and enjoyed the moment.

"Father."

At this, Josiah jumped slightly and laughed, opening his eyes and looking down to see his teenage daughter. "Mary, you startled me." He put the chairs down and hugged his daughter.

"I'm sorry." Mary smiled. She looked up and said, "You did jump a little." She laughed, and Josiah smiled and hugged her even more as he playfully growled at her. "Were you praying?" she asked and stepped back a bit, looking at her father while thinking she might have interrupted him.

"No. But I was enjoying what God has done for today," he said as he arranged the two chairs to point into the breeze. "Sit and let me show you." Mary sat down eagerly. She smiled, knowing what her father was about to do.

"Now, close your eyes, and tell me what he's done for us." Mary closed her eyes. She settled her hands in her lap, took in a deep breath, and let it out slowly. "Now, tell me, one at a time." Josiah almost whispered and leaned in toward her with his eyes closed.

"The sun feels nice and warm … and the breeze is cool, but not too cool."

"Good. What else?"

"I smell flowers. I should pick some for mother." Mary smiled, keeping her eyes closed; tilted her head back; and then turned slightly, as if trying to hear a distant sound.

"Keep going," Josiah said softly.

Mary paused and breathed deeply, turning her face toward the afternoon sun, which gave her face an amber glow. Josiah couldn't help but see Samira's facial features and smiled with pride at the young woman Mary had become.

"I smell cedar," Mary then said. "And I hear birds singing in the distance, and a rooster …"

"And the caravan is here, so there are things to gather and a donkey to load," Samira whispered into their ears while gently putting her hands on both their shoulders, smiling and pulling them together.

Mary jumped slightly as Josiah and Samira laughed. "Mother!" Mary cried out as she jumped off the chair and playfully pulled away. She spun in a circle and tried to cover her smile with her hands. "Mother, you scared me!" Mary began to laugh.

"She got you!" Josiah proclaimed, pointing at his daughter. Mary crinkled her nose and grunted, making funny faces at her father. Josiah reached out to grab her, but she just avoided him, grabbed one of the chairs, and ran toward a small corral. Josiah quickly grabbed the other chair and ran after her. Samira watched them playfully poking at each other, only slowing down when they entered the corral and approached the donkey.

Eiran, their hired worker, stood several feet away from the animal, not wanting to get any closer. "Master, I'm sorry." Eiran began to look down at the ground, feeling like a failure.

"It's okay, Eiran," Josiah said, patting his faithful servant on the back. "I couldn't have done any better." They both smiled.

Eiran had no family and had worked for Josiah and Samira for many years. He was old enough to be Josiah's father, and although he was a hired worker, he lived in their home, and Josiah trusted him with his life.

"Mary, I'm not even going to try this morning. You go ahead," her father said. Josiah said this donkey, named Sage, was the most stubborn animal in the land. Their battles were legendary. Mary seemed to be the only one who could subdue him. Occasionally, Josiah would go out to load him or plow, and the battle would begin. Sage would buck and bray, never giving an inch. Josiah would get a stick of wood and threaten Sage, but that's as far as it would go. The neighbors would laugh and joke with Josiah when they heard him call for Mary after threatening to take the donkey to Jerusalem and have him sacrificed.

"Good morning, Sage." Mary bowed to him like one would to royalty. "Permission to approach?"

"Mary, this is ridiculous," her father said as he rolled his eyes. "How many times do we have to go through this?"

Mary backed away from Sage and gestured to let her father try. "No, please," he sarcastically said, gesturing back to her with a bow.

"Now, Sage, we have work to do, and we need to load you up now." Sage just stood there as Mary approached him, and his skin shuddered when Mary ran her hand gently along his shoulder. He leaned into her touch, closed his eyes, and dropped his head. Mary nodded to Eiran, and he approached. Gently, she began to bridle the donkey. Josiah watched and shook his head in exasperation, cautiously approaching, and began to tie the chairs and a few baskets over the donkey's back.

"Here is one more," Samira quietly said as she walked into Sage's stall and handed over the last basket to Eiran. Mary had the reins and handed them to Eiran. Sage snorted in disapproval as Eiran led him across the courtyard toward the gate leading to the street.

"Mary, get the gate," Josiah said quietly, not wanting to entice the stubborn animal. "Samira, are you coming?" he asked. She had lingered back a few steps and stood on her toes, with both hands shielding her eyes from the sun, peering out toward the caravan. "There's no way you can see him from that distance," Josiah jested. "Come on; he's there. He said he'd be there."

"Mother, come on. Let's go!" Mary exclaimed. Grabbing her mother's hand, she pulled her through the gate, closing it behind them.

The caravan was coming from the hill country of Judea, and Samira looked forward to hearing from her family. Elizabeth and Zechariah, Samira's cousin and her husband, lived about a five-day journey away. They could only visit on special occasions, usually during feasts or Passover.

★★★

Mary wondered out loud, "Father, look how many camels there are. How many can there be?"

"More than one hundred, from what I can see," Josiah responded as they approached the camp. The traders came from all different countries, and if you didn't speak their language, it sometimes made it difficult to communicate. However, Josiah had picked up several different dialects over the years, and many of the traders had done the same. Josiah paused and turned toward Mary and Samira. "Mary, please remember what we discussed. The majority of these people are not Jewish, and they are very different from everyone in Nazareth. Make sure you do not speak to anyone, and do not look the men in the eye. Every land has different customs. Stay by my side at all times, and everything will be fine."

Mary said quietly, "Yes, Father," and then moved closer to her mother and adjusted her head covering.

Josiah nodded to Eiran; without speaking, he instinctively

understood his master's instructions to protect the women and stay alert.

As they approached the caravan, Mary was irritated and readjusted her scarf. "I don't understand why I have to cover my head, Mother. I'm pledged to Joseph, not married," Mary whispered to her mother. They both lowered their heads and followed respectfully behind Sage and the men.

"Often in life, we have to do things not for ourselves but for those around us. In this case, it's not so much about us as it is about them." Samira motioned to the groups of men unloading camels and setting up tents.

"Mary, watch the men unload the camels." Josiah motioned for them to stop, and they turned to watch a large group of camels lined up and a man standing beside every camel. They seemed to belong to a wealthy man who sat under an awning and was fanned by a young girl with a large palm leaf. The girl wasn't wearing much, and Mary was about to say something, but when she looked up and started to speak, her mother looked at her, and Mary knew not to say a word.

Suddenly, the wealthy man, dressed in purple, let out a loud shout, and one by one, the men pulled what looked like a string; instantly, everything fell off every camel to the ground. Mary clapped her hands quietly with a big smile. The man in purple laughed out loud and began to speak very quickly in a language Mary had never heard before.

"These men are Nabateans. They are from a very beautiful city called Raqmu. Some people call it Petra. It's carved into the side of a red cliff down a narrow passage. I was there when I was a young man. Very beautiful," Josiah reminisced.

"Josiah! My friend!" Josiah turned and was suddenly picked up off the ground by a huge man. Mary couldn't believe her eyes. He was nearly a cubit taller than her father, and he laughed and squeezed him while jumping up and down.

"Cn't brth … cn't brth … cn't brth." Josiah was trying to say something but struggled in the grasp of this giant.

Mary yelled, "Mother!" And at that moment, the giant man dropped Josiah to the ground, where he mumbled, "Can't breathe—couldn't breathe," shaking his head with a smile.

"You must be Mary," the giant said in a deep voice while turning toward Mary with a big smile.

Josiah yelled, "Don't do it, Ibrahim!" And he jumped on the giant's back, and they both began to laugh. Josiah dropped to the ground, and they continued to laugh as they embraced one another. "Mary, meet Ibrahim, the largest man I know." Mary was hiding behind Samira, trying to decide whether to come out.

Ibrahim spoke in a gentle voice and dropped down to one knee. "I'm sorry I've frightened you. It's a pleasure to meet you."

Mary came out from behind Samira with a new confidence and answered, "It's an honor to meet you." She moved to the side and surveyed the giant once again. "And now I know why the chairs we brought are so big," Mary said with a big smile, and they all laughed.

"Come, my friends. Let's have a meal together. The tent is already up, and the fire is ready," Ibrahim said. They all walked over to the tent. Eiran tied up Sage and began to remove the chairs.

"Here they are, just what you ordered." Josiah beamed with pride as Ibrahim sat down and tested the construction of his purchase. "You won't break these unless you drop them from the top of the temple." Josiah joked, and his friend handed him a small bag of silver coins. "Thank you, my friend. This is a blessing." Josiah joined him on one of the chairs.

"Thank you, Josiah. You're a good friend, and your wife is very restrained. She hasn't even asked me about Elizabeth and Zechariah."

"I'm not as restrained as you think, Ibrahim," Samira exclaimed from the side of the tent. "I'm simply being patient—very, very patient," she added as she brought a bowl of water for the men to wash up. Samira had dismissed the hired young man to water the camels. She and Mary had taken over the cooking and already had the first loaves over the hot rocks.

"Oh Lord, thank you, thank you, thank you. It smells so good. This new young man is a terrible cook, and he burns the bread almost every time," Ibrahim said, reaching out for one of the loaves.

"Don't you do it!" Samira said sternly from the washbasin behind him. Ibrahim's eyes widened as he pretended to be surprised by Samira's scolding. Mary washed her hands and laughed at their interaction.

They set out a wooden tray with fresh hot bread and some dried fish and olive oil. Everyone sat down, and Ibrahim prayed. "Blessed are you, and king of everything. All things come by your word. Amen."

"Amen," they all said together.

"Ibrahim, how is Atara?" Samira smiled and looked over, not realizing he hadn't heard a word she said.

Ibrahim had a full loaf torn open and held up to his nose. He shook his head back and forth, making a humming sound. Everyone at the table laughed at him, but he didn't have a care in the world.

"Ibrahim it's just bread," Josiah jested.

Ibrahim dropped his hands to his plate and said sternly, "Don't you tell me it's just bread, Master Josiah, the carpenter, who sleeps by his wife every night in his own bed, with fresh water and a fire burning all the time. Just bread?" Ibrahim looked around the table for sympathy and found none, so he began to pretend to cry and plea to Mary and Samira. "My dear ladies, do you not understand?" He pretended to sob, and Mary started to giggle. "You have no idea what I've been through." He sniffed twice with his best sad face on. "I have no warm bed at night, and the only thing that will keep my toes warm are the scorpions." He pointed at his giant dusty toes protruding from his sandals, which were probably a cubit in length. Mary half laughed and covered her eyes at the sight while Ibrahim quickly covered his feet with his tunic.

He continued but began to whisper, leaning in and looking around to see if anyone else was listening. "You see, this is not just bread. It's manna—manna from heaven." Josiah exhaled loudly, pretending to be annoyed, and leaned back on a sack of grain with his hands behind his head, preparing for a long tale.

"Now, you see …" The giant began to mumble, looking up toward the sky.

"Ibrahim, Atara … how is Atara?"

"Oh, yes, Atara … Atara … who is Atara?" Ibrahim asked, peering up toward the clear blue sky again, as if looking for the answer, while stuffing another partial loaf in his mouth.

Samira exclaimed, "Your wife!" She quickly grabbed the remaining bread from his hand and placed it on the table out of his immediate reach.

Ibrahim mumbled, "Okay, okay, I'm sorry." With a mouthful of bread, he settled back in his chair with a cup of wine. "Atara is doing very well, and she sends her love. She misses Nazareth, and I think we will return one day, when I grow weary of traveling day and night. However, I'm thinking you would like to know about Elizabeth and Zechariah."

As Ibrahim spoke, his whole demeanor changed, and he wasn't smiling anymore. "Samira, I did see Zechariah, but I did not see Elizabeth." He raised his hands before Samira could speak. "She's fine! She's fine. She didn't come outside, but Zechariah said she is fine. It was strange, though. Zechariah had lost his voice, and the people said he had an encounter with God when he was at the temple in Jerusalem; I'm not sure," Ibrahim said with uncertainty and hesitated. "I struggle to even repeat this, but people around the village were saying—"

"Were saying what?" Samira said, trying to contain herself.

"Well, they were saying Elizabeth is … is pregnant," he answered.

"Pregnant? That's crazy; she's too old to have a child," Samira protested.

"So was Sara," Josiah chided.

Samira seemed confused. "Josiah, this isn't funny. There's got to be some mistake. You know how people talk, always talking and gossiping about others. It's impossible."

"That's the craziest thing, Samira," Josiah interrupted. "I'm sure she's fine and there's an explanation. Maybe she just wasn't feeling well, and, like you said, people talk about anything and everything and make most of it up. We can go check on them in a few weeks. I'm sure everything is fine." Josiah leaned forward and took Samira's hand.

Samira began to gather the dishes, and Mary quickly jumped up and joined her. "Eiran, please get Sage. We need to go. It's getting late. Thank you for the news, Ibrahim." Samira forced a smile as she took the last of the leftover food into the tent.

"Josiah, I'm sorry. I didn't mean to—"

"It's all right, my friend. I'm sure everything is fine. Thank you for the meal. It's so good to see you again, but it is getting dark," Josiah said and motioned for Eiran to depart.

"Samira, I'm sorry. I didn't mean to upset you," Ibrahim said as he tied a sack of grain onto the donkey.

"It's all right. I'm fine. Thank you for the meal and the grain. Please tell Atara I'll be waiting on her return." Samira smiled, grabbed Mary's hand, and walked toward Sage and Eiran. Mary turned around and waved, walking backward for a few steps.

"Josiah, my friend …" Ibrahim started.

"It's all right. Thank you, my friend. I will see you in a few months." They both embraced, and Josiah smiled and waved, running to catch up with his family.

"You know, Zechariah and Elizabeth serve God and are blessed." Josiah comforted his wife after catching up with them.

"I know. It's just not like her to stay hidden and not come out and speak to Ibrahim. You're right. I'm sure everything is fine," Samira responded with a smile for Josiah's sake. Josiah kissed her on the cheek and joined Eiran as they walked back through the caravan toward home.

Mary put an arm around Samira. "Mother, do you think it's possible for Elizabeth to have a child at her age? Father was right. Sara had a baby when she was old. I'm going to have a baby when Joseph comes for me."

"Maybe so," Samira mumbled, staring into the distance, not comprehending what Mary said. "Maybe so."

CHAPTER 3

The sun was just beginning to set in the desert sky when Josiah and his family got back to the gate of the family home. "I'll get it," Mary announced, running ahead to open the gate.

Samira walked through the gate toward the dwindling fire. "I will start some food." She smiled at Josiah as she passed him, and he knew she was all right.

Mary ran by and quickly grabbed the donkey's reins from Eiran. "Here, let me," she said. Eiran swatted at her as she ran by, leading Sage back to the corral.

"Mary!" Josiah protested.

"Sorry, Eiran," Mary apologized. But she knew Eiran didn't care. He was like a grandfather to her, and they were close.

"It's okay, Josiah. She's young. Remember what that was like?" Eiran put his arm around Josiah's shoulder. They both laughed and walked into the corral.

"Shalom! May I come in?" A voice came from beyond the wall.

Someone was already unlatching the gate when Josiah looked over and answered, "Well, hello, Joseph."

"Shalom," Joseph said to the two men and embraced each of them. Eiran, being the elder, embraced Joseph and kissed him on his forehead.

Suddenly, time seemed to stand still as Joseph just stopped, looked at Mary, and then awkwardly looked at Josiah, not wanting to greet her presumptuously without permission. Josiah motioned toward Mary, giving Joseph permission to greet his daughter.

"Hello, Mary," Joseph said in a rigid manner, not wanting to appear weak before the men. Josiah and Eiran smiled and shook their heads at his clumsy attempt at chivalry.

Mary and Joseph had known each other since they were children. Joseph was a little older, but their families both agreed they were a match from the beginning, and it was a plus that they really seemed to care for one another.

Before Mary could respond, Josiah said, "Mary, if you will excuse us, we have a matter to discuss."

Mary smiled hugely and suddenly realized Joseph was here to make arrangements for the conclusion of their wedding. "Oh!" Mary almost shouted. "Yes, Father, I will. Uh, Mother, I mean …" Mary stammered and walked sideways past the men as she gestured toward the stairs leading to the roof, her face now bright red. "I'll just go now. Bye." She turned around and ran, yelling, "Mother!" All three men laughed as she vanished up the stairs, climbing two at a time.

According to Jewish law, a betrothed couple signs a marriage contract. After the dowry is paid, the couple remains separated until the groom prepares a place for the bride. Only then does he come back to receive her to consummate their union. Joseph had come to make those final arrangements.

"Well, young man, are you ready?" Josiah faced Joseph with a hand on each shoulder.

"I am, sir. All the arrangements are made, and I would like to come for her in two days—with your permission, of course," Joseph said with reassuring confidence.

"Now, there is the man I am giving my daughter to." Josiah embraced him and said, "Blessed are you, son of Heli. Blessed are you, coming and going. You are blessed in the field and in the city. Blessed is the fruit of your loins—a long life, and many sons. Amen."

"Amen," Eiran repeated.

Josiah led them to some stone seats around the fire pit. "Come; let's celebrate! Samira, let's have some wine." Josiah called to her on the roof.

"Coming right down!" she shouted back.

Samira had gone up to get some spices she had set out to dry when she heard Mary yell for her. Mary came running up the stairs, excited and laughing but also embarrassed. Tears began to stream down her face by the time she got to her mother. She almost knocked Samira over as she hugged her tightly.

Samira asked, "Isn't it exciting?" She pulled Mary's scarf down, pushed her hair back, and wiped the tears from her face. "Now, now, you're a woman now, and your husband is coming for you. It's a wonderful gift from God." They sat down together on a large pile of straw, Mary's head lying across Samira's lap.

"I was excited until now. Now, I'm scared. What's it like, Mother?" Mary had stopped crying and lay on her back, staring at the stars while she played with strands of her mother's long hair.

"It's a beautiful, wondrous experience to be shared only by you and Joseph," Samira said, wiping the last of the tears from Mary's face. "Look at me. I'm proud of you, Mary." She cupped her daughter's face in her hands. "I'm proud of the woman you have become. You will be a good wife and a good mother." Samira began to get up, and Mary rolled over, gazing out over the moonlit desert. "Are you going to stay up here tonight?"

"I think so," Mary replied.

"Okay. Get some rest."

"Samira!" Josiah called again from downstairs.

"Coming," she responded after getting to the bottom of the stairs to join them.

Mary stretched in the straw and counted shooting stars until she fell asleep.

Apparently, she slept for quite some time, because when she woke up, the moon was higher in the sky, and the house was quiet. She stirred a bit and rolled over, not wanting to wake up, but something pulled her from her slumber. She sighed and sat up, rubbing her eyes, and saw a glowing light all around her. It seemed to get brighter and brighter, yet it didn't get brighter; it got closer. She had never seen anything like it. It seemed thick, as if she could almost touch it. She reached out with her hand to touch her arm. Her whole body glowed and felt warm. It felt almost like being in a warm pool of water, but she wasn't wet.

"Mary."

She looked up and was paralyzed with fear. She tried to scream, but nothing came out. There, in front of her, was what looked like a man. He was two cubits taller than Ibrahim, and she realized the light was coming from this man. Her feet started moving as she crawled backward to the corner of the wall, pushing piles of straw up against the wall. Somehow, she knew he wouldn't hurt her, but his enormous size and the light unsettled her to her core.

"Rejoice. You are highly favored, and the Lord is with you. You are blessed among women." His voice had a deepness and a power as she had never heard before. His greeting confused her, and she began to tremble.

"I am Gabriel, a messenger from the Most High," he continued. "Do not be afraid, Mary. You have found favor with God." Mary sat up and immediately felt peace like never before. She knew the words he said were true. "You will conceive in your womb, and you will have a son, and you will name him Jesus. He will be called Great and the Son of the Most High. The Lord God will give him the throne of his father, David. He will reign over the house of Jacob forever, and his kingdom will have no end."

Mary felt at ease and spoke to the angel. "How can I have a child when I haven't been with a man?"

Gabriel responded, "The Holy Spirit will touch you, and the power of the Highest will overshadow you, and the Holy One who will be born will be called the Son of God. It is also true that your cousin, Elizabeth, is pregnant in her old age. She was barren, but with God, all things are possible."

Mary stood, looked up at him, and said, "I will be the maidservant of the Lord." She bowed her head and said, "Please let it be as you have spoken."

When she opened her eyes, he was gone. At that point, sleep was gone. She would sit up and pray, and she couldn't wait to tell her father in the morning.

★★★

"Mary ... Mary, surely you're not still asleep!" Samira called from downstairs.

Josiah went up to check on her and found her curled up in the straw, sound asleep. Josiah sat beside her and gently rubbed her arm. "Hey, sleepy."

As he spoke, Mary rolled over with her eyes closed and stretched. She curled back up, resting her head on her father's lap. "Father, the most wonderful thing happened last night," Mary mumbled in a groggy voice.

"And what would that be?" Josiah asked while he removed pieces of straw from her hair.

"Father, an angel was here last night, and he talked to me about a baby ... a king." Mary sat up, slowly opened her eyes, and looked at her father. "I'm going to have a baby."

Josiah smiled and hugged her as he brushed off more straw, saying, "Well, of course, you are. That's what wives hope to do."

"But—" she tried to explain.

"Mary, you can tell me about your dream later."

"Father, it wasn't a—"

"The roosters have been up half the day, and your mother could use your help while we still have you." Josiah stood up and pulled Mary up, hugging her. "I love you, Mary, and I'm so proud of you."

"I love you too, Father, but I need to—"

"We can talk later. Now go!" he said half-jokingly, gently pushing her toward the stairs.

"Yes, Father." Mary looked back at him with a look he hadn't seen before—an adult look.

"Hey, hey, come here. What's wrong?"

"Father, I'm … pregnant." Mary took her father's hand and looked at him with excitement. "The angel told me—"

"Mary, don't be silly. That can't be true." Josiah stepped a few steps away from her and, looking at her, waited for her to begin laughing. Mary looked at him, and Josiah knew they would have no banter between them this morning.

Samira had been listening from the stairs and slowly stepped up and looked at Josiah. "Samira, talk to her. This isn't funny." Josiah nervously took his wife's arm and pulled her closer to Mary.

"Mother, an angel appeared to me last night and told me I would … I would …" Mary's face grew pale, and she ran to the railing on the roof and threw up over the edge. She looked back at her parents, panting and wiping her face with the scarf draped over her shoulders. Josiah and Samira froze, and neither one could move nor speak. Josiah slowly fell forward onto his hands and knees, feeling sick himself.

"What have you done?" Josiah mumbled. His head was spinning, and his face began to turn deep red. "What have you done!" Josiah screamed at Mary, trying to get to his feet. "Do you have any idea—?"

"Father, please … let me …" Mary couldn't believe her father didn't believe her. She began to cry and move toward him.

"Don't. Don't you dare," he said, putting a hand out, motioning for her to stop. Samira sat on the ground, crying with both hands covering her face.

"Eiran! Eiran!"

"Yes, Josiah." Eiran had been waiting at the bottom of the stairs when he heard the commotion.

"Get Joseph. Get him *now!*"

"Yes, Josiah, I'm leaving now."

"Hurry!" Josiah yelled.

As Eiran opened the gate, he saw Joseph running toward him. He also saw many of the neighbors standing on their roofs, all watching to see what the commotion was all about.

"What's wrong, Eiran?" Joseph was worried and out of breath. He became even more so when Eiran wouldn't look him in the eye.

"Josiah wants you on the roof." Eiran looked at the ground as he held the gate open.

"Eiran, what is going on?"

Joseph ran across the courtyard in a panic and had just reached the top of the stairs when Josiah grabbed him and pushed him against the clay and brick wall, asking, "What have you done?"

Joseph looked past Josiah and saw Mary and Samira both collapsed on the ground, crying. Mary clenched her fists, crying, "Please, Father, don't. Please." Her eyes were swollen, and she reached out to her mother. "Mother, please do something."

"Josiah, what is going on?" Joseph asked.

Josiah gritted his teeth, just staring at Joseph, when Mary stood up and screamed, "It wasn't him; it wasn't him! That's what I've been trying to tell you. Joseph didn't make me pregn—" Josiah put his hand over her mouth and pulled her down to the ground. He had also seen the people gathering on their roofs. Under Jewish law, adultery, even with a marriage contract, meant Mary would be stoned to death.

"Pregnant … pregnant?" That's all Joseph could say as he slid down the wall and sat on the ground with a blank stare.

Josiah sat holding Mary and began to cry. "Mary, why … why would you do this?"

"Father, please listen. Let me explain."

Eiran had come to the roof and now witnessed the chaos and flurry of emotion. Not knowing exactly what to do, he slowly approached Josiah, knelt down, and quietly said in his ear, "Josiah, you need to get yourself together. We must do something now!"

Josiah looked up, confused. He looked at Eiran as if he didn't know him and, through the emotions and confusion, realized what he said. "Eiran." Josiah shook his head and paused for a moment to collect his thoughts. He stared at the clay floor and began to get up. Mary just lay there crying as Eiran helped him up. Josiah wiped his face with his tunic, holding on to Eiran's arm to steady himself.

"Thank you, my friend," Josiah said, looking around and surveying the crowd beginning to gather in the street. "Go quickly, and get provisions. Take Sage, and get her to Zechariah and Elizabeth's. Use the back entrance. We will stay up here." Josiah walked over to Samira and pulled her to her feet. She went limp in his arms, sobbing and trying to hang on to him. "Samira, please, Mary's life depends on us now.

"Joseph, get up. Get up now!" Josiah said. Joseph just sat there with a blank stare, and Josiah pulled him up and sat him on a wooden bench near the wall. "Joseph, if you ever loved her, please do as I ask." Joseph nodded in affirmation as he hung his head and stared down at the clay roof. "All you have to do is sit here where they can see you. Stay here!" Josiah spoke and moved with a sense of urgency, fully realizing what was immediately at stake. He stooped down out of sight and ran over to Mary. He gently grabbed her and sat her up.

"Father, if you would just listen … please, you know me," Mary begged, pulling with both hands on the front of her father's tunic. Josiah was moved but realized time was short. The Jewish people were very zealous about the law, and it seemed some of them might have heard what was said in the heat of the discussion.

"Mary, there is no time for this. I love you, and it doesn't matter." Josiah began to cry, holding his daughter tight when he felt them getting pulled apart. Eiran had returned, and he tried to lift Mary to her feet.

"We must go now," Eiran insisted, gently pulling her up. Josiah broke down crying and grabbed Mary's hands. Their grasp was only broken when Eiran pulled her backward toward the stairs.

Mary cried so hard she could barely speak. "I love you; don't do this." She struggled to get the words and reached back for them both. "Mother, please ... Joseph!" She was only quieted as Eiran gently covered her mouth with her scarf and carried her down the stairs and out the back of the house.

Josiah crawled over to Samira, and they sat there crying for a time.

★★★

It took Mary and Eiran several days to get to the hill country of Judea. Zechariah and Elizabeth were outside and saw them coming up the dusty hill toward their house. Mary was overwhelmed with emotion when she saw Elizabeth, and she jumped off Sage and ran the rest of the way toward her older cousin. Mary smiled for the first time in days when she got close enough to see Elizabeth was pregnant. They both laughed when they embraced, because at that very moment, Elizabeth's baby kicked so intensely that they both could feel it. They held hands and walked up the road toward the house.

It was getting dark. After talking for a while with Zechariah, Mary and Elizabeth sat up most of the night talking through what had taken place, trying to make sense of it all.

As the sun began to rise, Mary took a walk to pray and spend time with the Lord. The sun was just spilling over the Judean hills and spreading across the valley below. Mary closed her eyes and just stood there, struggling with the pain of the past few days and her desire to understand what God was doing. After a long while, she whispered, "Lord, what have you done for me today?"

With eyes closed, a single tear rolled down her cheeks. She

instinctively reached out as if to hold her father's hand. "The sun is warm but not too warm. There is a gentle breeze." Mary smiled and turned her face upward.

She felt sadness and joy, and she could almost hear her father ask, "What else?"

"I hear the roosters and an ox or donkey coming this way on the road." She stayed very still, listening to the sound getting closer and closer, and then it stopped. Mary's eyes opened, and there, she saw Joseph standing with his donkey. They just stood there, neither of them knowing what to say.

Joseph took a step forward, and Mary backed up a step. Joseph stopped and raised his hand, reaching out for her. "Mary, please forgive me. I know you're hurt."

She just stood there confused, not knowing how to respond. Her heart was broken because he hadn't believed her, but her prayer wouldn't leave her mind, and the words overwhelmed her: "Lord, what have you done for me today?"

"Mary, the angel appeared to me too. I understand now." He took a step closer, and she didn't move away. "I know the child is from God." Joseph came two steps closer and could almost reach her. "I want to go home." He reached down slowly and gently took her hand. "I want to bring my wife"—she hesitated when he gently pulled her his direction—"and our child." Joseph saw her countenance soften, and he reached for her, picked her up, and sat her on the donkey.

★★★

Joseph took Mary back to Nazareth as his wife, and they stayed there for several months. Even though they were married according to the law by the signing of the contract, Mary becoming pregnant before the traditional time was frowned upon, and for a time, they felt like outcasts when they attended synagogue and went to the market.

It was actually a welcome event when the Roman government called for a census to count the people in their provinces. Because Joseph was from Bethlehem, he and Mary traveled there nearing the time of Jesus's birth. The little town was crowded because of the census, so people slept in the streets and tents, having come from all over. Joseph met a man who was kind enough to let he and Mary stay with their animals, and that's where Jesus was born.

One day, a voice called out from the courtyard of the home: "Joseph!"

"Good morning, Greitus." Joseph stepped out of the corral and embraced the owner of the property. "Is everything okay?" Joseph asked when he saw the curious expression on Greitus's face.

"Well, yes … um, you have some visitors." Just as Greitus spoke, Joseph saw a group of men entering the courtyard. Three of them were dressed in the finest silk garments, and their servants followed respectfully. They looked as if they might be from Nabatea, or possibly Decapolis.

The first man spoke with an accent. "We are here to see the child."

"What business do you have with us and our son?" Joseph asked defensively.

"Please forgive our intrusion." The second man spoke up with a slightly different accent. He gestured to the servants, and they brought three wooden boxes, opened them, and placed them on the ground at Joseph's feet. This astonished both Joseph and Greitus. The first two boxes contained very expensive spices of frankincense and myrrh, and gold coins filled the last box.

Finally, the last of the three man spoke up. "These gifts are for the child. He will be a king one day, and we have come to pay tribute to him." Joseph just stood there, confused and a little frightened, staring at the open boxes. "Please, my name is Balthazar, and this is King Gaspar, and King Melchior. May we see him? We have traveled a great distance."

"Oh yes, of course. Please come this way." Joseph knew

they meant no harm, but the whole thing overwhelmed him. The servants quickly collected the boxes and laid them open on the ground in front of the manger, where little Jesus slept. They quickly moved back out of the way, and the three kings bowed down several times on their knees. They each began to speak quietly, possibly praying in their own languages. They quickly stood up and bowed to both Joseph and Mary, thanked them, and departed.

Greitus, Joseph, and Mary sat there with the animals, staring at the boxes, not knowing what to say until Greitus finally broke the uncomfortable silence. "Well, I'll ... just go. I have some things. We can talk later."

Joseph just looked up in a stupor and waved, not knowing what to say. Mary began to smile, stood up, and took Joseph by the arm, saying, "God has provided for his son." Joseph looked at her and hugged her, and they both began to laugh.

They both had trouble getting to sleep that night, and as soon as Joseph fell asleep, he was warned in a dream that King Herod was coming to kill the child and he had to take his family to Egypt immediately. When Joseph woke up from the dream, he told Mary what they had to do. So they packed their things, loaded their donkey, and left for Egypt that night.

In Egypt, Joseph worked as a carpenter. They stayed there until King Herod died and it was safe to return to Nazareth. When they returned home, they settled into daily life, and the painful events of a few years before dissolved with time. Jesus learned carpentry from Joseph and learned to read and write from the scrolls that Joseph purchased with some of the gold the kings had brought to them.

CHAPTER 4

Jesus's childhood was much like that of any other boy growing up in Nazareth. He did chores, studied the holy scrolls, played games with his friends, and lived a life like any normal Jewish child. However, his unique ability to learn, memorize, and understand the written law set him apart. No greater example of this occurred than the time he traveled to Jerusalem for the feast of Passover.

Joseph took Mary and Jesus to the Holy City with a large group from Nazareth. It was dangerous to travel the roads alone because thieves would wait to hold up small groups or single travelers, so most people traveled the roads together in large groups.

Joseph and the group from Nazareth arrived early and stayed with others outside the city walls near the Gihon Spring. People often waited for hours near a water source during Passover just to get enough water for drinking and cooking. Joseph had also witnessed many disputes and fights, so he picked this spot near the Gihon Spring to avoid any altercations.

When Joseph and Jesus went to the temple, they purchased a healthy lamb without any blemishes or spots for the sacrifice. Jesus carefully carried it back to their tent, tied it up carefully, and gave it some water.

After several days of going back and forth into Jerusalem for the Passover celebration, the group from Nazareth headed out of the city to pack their things and gather supplies for the long trip back to Nazareth. As Jesus walked close to Mary and brushed his hand along the outer wall of the temple, he spoke quietly. Mary could barely make out what he said.

"Blessed are you, Jonas, son of Nar, and blessed is your family for the work you have done on this temple. Blessed are you, Timothy, and your sense of humor that blessed those around you while you carved this block." When Jesus said this, he smiled at the thought and continued. Mary just listened and wondered why he was praying in this way. "Blessed are you, Asher, son of Zev, for the sacrifice you made to build this temple—"

Mary interrupted. "Jesus, who are you praying for?" She pulled him close and walked beside him.

"The men who built the temple, Mother!" Jesus looked up, excited to tell her about what he was doing.

"That's a nice thing to do, but all of this was built before you were born, and it sounded like you were calling them by name."

Jesus took his mother's hand and casually responded, "Of course, I was."

Mary took a few steps and stopped and turned to look at him when she realized what he had said. "But how could you?"

Jesus exclaimed, "It's okay, Mother. Come on!" He tugged on her hand, trying to run to catch up with the others. "Come on!" Jesus smiled and ran ahead. Mary just smiled and waved at him.

From time to time, Jesus amazed Mary and Joseph with his understanding of the law, and then, other times, he would say or do things that she and Joseph didn't understand. Today was one of those times.

Jesus was with a group of boys toward the back when the caravan stopped for water at the last pool before they traveled away from Jerusalem. He was walking by the last gate to the city when something caught his attention. All the way down at the end of the street, something was going on. Jesus slowly walked toward the gate, intrigued by the commotion.

Some of the other boys called to him. "Jesus, come on!"

"Okay, in a minute," he responded, but he changed direction and walked back toward the temple. By this time, the caravan was out of sight, and no one even knew he had gone missing.

After a day and a half of travel, Mary began to look for Jesus. She and Joseph hadn't seen him, and they assumed he was with friends or part of the family. She checked up and down the caravan of people and didn't feel worried until she reached Joseph in the front and said in a panic, "I can't find Jesus. Joseph, I've checked with everyone."

Joseph cried out to the men in front, "Stop the caravan!"

Everyone slowly came to a halt as Joseph checked with each family from the front to the back. Finally, he spoke with the boys Jesus had been with when they left the city. Then Joseph ran back to the front and announced, "He's in Jerusalem. I'll need some others to go with us!"

Six families volunteered, which gave them a large-enough group to make it difficult for the thieves on the road.

They had split away from the group and were headed back toward the city when Joseph heard a man call out, "Hey, wait." Joseph turned around and saw another family hurrying to join them. As the man with his wife and son caught up, he asked, out of breath, "Hello, Joseph? I'm Seth, and this is my wife, Yona, and our son, Nathaniel. We were moving to Nazareth, and we'd like to help you find your son."

The men embraced briefly, and Mary began to cry when Yona put an arm around her and told her, "Everything will be fine. Yahweh will protect him."

"I know." Mary smiled through the tears. "Thank you."

Back in the city, Jesus stood in the middle of the street, watching what looked like the high priest and his disciples walking toward him near the temple entrance. They got closer, and the crowd moved to make way for the group, but Jesus remained still in the middle of the street, taking in the spectacle.

Children clamored for attention and laughed as the high priest threw dates and grapes to them. The way the high priest waved to the parents and those passing by made it obvious he was trying to be seen. And he couldn't help but be distracted by the one young man standing in the street, just staring at him. He seemed to grow more and more distracted and even irritated as he got closer and closer to Jesus.

As he approached Jesus, the high priest threw the rest of the fruit off to the side, and the children all ran after it, except Jesus.

"Good morning," Jesus said respectfully.

"Well, good morning, young man. Do I know you?"

"No, I'm certain we have never met," Jesus responded with a pleasant smile.

"Well, let me introduce myself. I'm Annas—"

"Yes, I know. The high priest! Forgive my interruption," Jesus said as he looked at the high priest's disciples, who seemed displeased and ready to make an example out of him. Annas raised his hand toward them.

"No, it's quite all right. What's your name?" Annas continued, recognizing this young man had something very different about him than other boys his age.

"I'm Jesus, Jesus of Nazareth," he said with the same smile.

"Well, maybe I know your father."

"No, High Priest, I'm very sure you don't know him."

Annas spoke with a forced smile while he looked around at the crowd. "How could you possibly know that?"

"High Priest, my father and I are of the same house. He is always near me, and I am always near him. I would know if he had met you." Jesus spoke with confidence, angering the group of disciples even more.

Annas raised his hand toward his disciples once more. "Well, young Jesus of Nazareth, you are a peculiar young man. Are you of age to enter the temple?"

"I am."

The disciples yelled, "Blasphemy!" while grabbing at Jesus.

Annas raised his voice angrily. "Release him! He's a young man and probably doesn't even know what he said. Jesus, 'I Am' is the response Yahweh gave Moses when he asked him his name on the mountain."

Jesus just looked at him and simply responded, "Yes, High Priest."

Annas looked at him for a moment, trying to discern if he had admitted he knew what he was saying or he had received the correction. Annas just shook his head in exasperation. "All right, come, and we can talk."

The high priest introduced Jesus to a young man walking directly beside him. "By the way, this is Caiaphas. He will soon be my son-in-law." Caiaphas looked Jesus up and down, taking note of his simple clothing and sandals. When Jesus said hello, he just glared at him in disgust. Annas watched their interaction and simply smiled. "Come with us, young Jesus. We will teach you about the law for Nazareth's sake."

All the high priest's disciples laughed. Jesus just smiled and followed them into the temple courts. As the high priest made his way through the temple courts, Sadducees and Pharisees stopped what they were doing and followed Annas and his disciples.

Jesus slept in the temple and listened and asked questions there for two days. He rose early on the third day, washed his hands and face, and joined the group gathered around the high priest. They were settled in a large covered area when Annas began to speak. "Good morning, everyone. I would like to introduce my friend who has been with us for a few days. This is young Jesus, Jesus of Nazareth. He is of age and has come to further his learning about the law and the prophets." Everyone nodded in agreement, and those close to him encouraged him.

"I know, my brothers, we have disagreed in the past about a great many things, but one thing we all agree on is the law was given to Moses by Yahweh." Annas stood up and began to get louder and more flamboyant as he spoke. "The law is life itself, and to stray away from it and to place too much emphasis on the prophets and the Messiah's coming will lead to a disruption in everyday life as we know it. I believe the Messiah will come one day, and I believe what the prophets wrote has some truth to it. But let us reason together, brothers, like men. The law, and the keeping of the law, should be our main concern!"

Some of the Sadducees shouted, "Amen," while most of the Pharisees grumbled and made comments under their breath.

Caiaphas stood up and took the floor. "I agree, High Priest! Did Moses not write, 'If you fully obey the Lord your God and carefully follow all his commands I give you today, the Lord your God will set you high above all the nations on earth'? Did he not?" Caiaphas began to get louder, and the Sadducees encouraged him while he strutted around, stirring them up. "Did Moses not write, 'Know therefore that the Lord your God is God; he is a faithful God, keeping his covenant of love to a thousand generations of those who love him and keep his commandments'?'"

Some of the men shouted, "Yes, yes, he did. Amen!"

"Then why do we spend our time focusing on the prophets and waste time on things like the afterlife when the law is where we should spend our time? Why? Why do we, Jesus of Nazareth?" Caiaphas half bowed to Jesus mockingly and quickly took a seat right in front of him. "This should be good," Caiaphas told another young Sadducee, and they both laughed.

Jesus slowly stood up and looked out at all the teachers, young and old. He walked out into the center of the circle to complete silence. All eyes were on him. Two of the Pharisees, Nicodemus and Joseph of Arimathea, knew that Caiaphas was trying to make Jesus look bad. They were about to stand up and object when Jesus began to speak.

Jesus spoke and motioned with his hands toward Caiaphas. "Would you all also agree that the law is the foundation of our faith?"

Caiaphas just stared at him with disdain and finally answered, "Yes, we would."

Then Jesus said, "Yahweh has built on that foundation, giving us the writings and the words of the prophets. Did Moses not say, 'I will raise up for them a prophet like you from among their brethren, and will put my words in his mouth, and he shall speak to them all that I command him'? Are we to cast aside the words of the Lord our God because a prophet other than Moses spoke them? And did Solomon not instruct us to pursue wisdom and understanding at all costs?" Jesus spoke with authority, and his impossibly advanced understanding of the Holy Scriptures amazed everyone in the crowd.

He continued as he stood still in the middle of the circle. "If our pursuit of wisdom is a roof, and the prophets are the walls laid on the foundation of the law, how can we cast aside the walls that support the roof? Do they not all work together?"

Joseph of Arimathea spoke up, and he and some of the Pharisees applauded, saying, "They do."

By this time, Caiaphas was red in the face and getting angrier as each moment passed.

One of the Pharisees asked, "Jesus, what is your opinion about the afterlife?" The Sadducees groaned because they didn't believe in an afterlife, and they hotly debated this topic with the Pharisees.

"I have no opinion, and I can only repeat to you what the Holy Scriptures say." Jesus walked toward Joseph of Arimathea and spoke directly to him and Nicodemus. "In the garden, there were two trees: the tree of life, which Adam and Eve had free access to, and the tree of the knowledge of good and evil, which they chose. If Yahweh put the tree of life in the garden for them to freely eat from and then banished them from the garden so they would not eat from it and live forever in a sinful state, then it would appear that his original intent was for man to live forever with him. Also, King David wrote of this life, 'You will counsel me and receive me into glory afterward, who do I have in heaven, but you?' Do we not believe even Moses, when he said, 'Those that sleep in the earth will awake, some to everlasting life, and some to everlasting contempt'?"

When Jesus said that, he looked straight at Caiaphas and motioned with his hands, welcoming a response. No one said a word. Everyone was astonished, and even Annas wasn't sure what to say. Jesus then looked up and saw a young man from the caravan at the outer edge of the circle motioning for him to come over.

Just as Jesus was about to excuse himself, Caiaphas jumped up and said, "Rabbis, teachers, have we come to this? Are we really going to sit here and listen to the words of a boy from Nazareth?" Some of them started to grumble, and Caiaphas continued. "We have studied for years, and I, for one, am guided by *my* understanding of scripture, and that is what leads *my* path … That is what leads *our* path!" Caiaphas shouted.

They began to say, "Amen, amen. Blessed be the Lord forever." Caiaphas sat back down and straightened his expensive silk garments after making his point.

Jesus looked at Annas and raised both his hands to quiet the crowd. "High Priest, thank you for allowing me to come and share. I have truly learned a lot." He nodded toward Annas and began to walk out when he suddenly turned and spoke with an intensity that startled some of them. "Caiaphas! King David also wrote"—Jesus paused and looked intently at him—"'Trust in the Lord with all your heart, and lean not on your own understanding; rather, in all you do, acknowledge him, and he will direct your path'!"

Jesus looked over at Nicodemus and Joseph of Arimathea, who sat back and smiled, and many of the disciples clapped as Jesus walked out, taking the young man's hand.

Caiaphas was furious but had no words. He would remember this day and the name Jesus of Nazareth.

Then, the young man from the caravan said to Jesus, "Come

quickly; your parents are looking for you!" So they began to run toward the outer courts.

★★★

When she saw her son, Mary yelled, "Jesus!" and ran to hug him. She wept openly when she reached out for him and held him close. "Jesus, my son, why, why have you done this to us? We've been worried, looking everywhere for you." Mary knelt down, holding him tightly, and Jesus looked down, took her face in his hands, and wiped the tears from her face.

"Mother, why were you looking for me? Didn't you realize I had to be in my Father's house?" As Jesus comforted her, Mary heard the words of the angel Gabriel ringing in her ears as she looked at him: "'You will conceive in your womb, and you will have a son, and you will name him Jesus. He will be called great and will be called the Son of the Most High. The Lord God will give him the throne of his father David. He will reign over the house of Jacob forever, and his kingdom will have no end'"

By this time, the whole group had joined together, and everyone was relieved to find Jesus unharmed. The men joked that there were worse things than spending three days learning from the high priest in the temple. They all walked out together and headed toward the donkeys tied up outside the temple. As they reached the dusty road outside of Jerusalem, the breeze picked up. A few clouds rolled in to cool at least the first part of their journey.

That day, Joseph of Arimathea and Nicodemus walked out of the temple together, neither of them saying a word. Finally, Nicodemus broke the silence. "There is something extraordinary about that young man."

"Yes, there is, and it's not just his knowledge or his ability to reason and draw the text together, as he does, although that is extraordinary for any twelve-year-old," Joseph added. They stopped and looked at each other. "There is something more about him—something that you can't touch, Nicodemus."

"Yes, you're right—something we need to keep an eye on." They both chuckled and walked out into the streets of Jerusalem. The sun was going down, and people were hurrying to get home.

"Good night, my friend," Joseph called out as they walked in opposite directions. Nicodemus waved and walked up the hill toward his home.

CHAPTER 5

"Nathaniel, you are up early today."

Nathaniel said hesitantly, "Yes, Father, I thought I would get an early start on my chores. I wanted to go see Jesus."

"Well, first, let's eat breakfast, and then we can talk about the rest of the day."

The boy slumped in his chair and got ready for the "you're a man now, and it's time to take responsibility and prepare for your future, and you need to work on your skills as a carpenter" speech. Nathaniel was getting older and wanted to be with his friends. He wanted to go down to the market and see if any of the village girls were there helping sell their families' goods.

"Thank you, Mother," he said. Yona had placed some fresh bread on the table. Nathaniel looked up and half smiled, feeling his mother knew what he was about to endure.

"You know, Nathaniel, you're a man now, and you should be concerned with your future and perfecting your skill as a carpenter," Seth said without looking up. Nathaniel looked up at his mother in hopes that she might rescue him. Yona smiled and insistently pointed to his food.

Nathaniel nodded and responded, "Yes, Father, but even Joseph said I'm one of the best carpenters he's seen. He said I have a gift, and I know it's because of the hard work and practice, but—"

"But nothing," his father interrupted. "Son, you know I love you. I remember what it's like to be your age, wanting to go with your friends and to experience adventure." Seth paused for a moment, staring out the window as if reliving a moment from his youth.

Nathaniel looked up with hope in his eyes. "Yes, Father, that's it!" But the feeling quickly faded when his father continued.

"But we have a responsibility to God and to your future family to become the best we can be. And that takes practice. Your mother and I won't be here forever, and when we are gone, this will all be yours. You have to take responsibility and become a good businessman. Nathaniel, why don't you finish up and go sweep the shop."

"But I already—"

"Nathaniel!" Yona was insistent, and she winked at him when he looked up.

"Oh, yes, Mother." Nathaniel jumped up, grabbed a large piece of flatbread, and hurried out the door.

Yona scurried around the kitchen and hummed her favorite Jewish song of praise. Seth sat there and slowly ate his breakfast, fully aware of what his wife was doing. After a few moments, Seth sighed loudly and pushed his partially eaten plate of food to the middle of the table. "Yona, I know what you're doing," Seth conceded.

"I'm sure I don't know what you're talking about."

"Defender, oh defender of my son—" Seth said playfully.

"*Our* son!" Yona interjected.

"I'm sorry, defender and advocate of *our* son. Please present your case."

Seth playfully pounded his fist on the table, and Yona stopped what she was doing and sat across from him. She said playfully, "With your permission, most-high judge, I would like to ask you some questions."

Seth sat in an arrogant posture, adjusted his tunic, and said, "You may begin."

"First, I would like to ask you, is Nathaniel a wise, responsible young man?"

"He is. Please continue." He sat up straight, eyeing her cautiously.

"And would you agree he is not only a great carpenter but perhaps even a better carpenter than you?"

He agreed. "It is possible. I am a great teacher."

Yona just nodded and smiled. "And would you agree that, because of your *great teaching*, the young man in question would make a great husband and father, even now?" Yona leaned forward and looked at him intently.

When Seth looked into her piercing hazel eyes, he couldn't help but pause and admire the same wisdom, love, and tenacity that drew him to her when they met. "I have to agree that that might be true ... only because of my great teaching." They both began to laugh.

Yona stood up and walked behind him, draping her arms around his shoulders and chest, and leaned in close. This time, she spoke softly as a wife. "Then is it possible that the real reason you're keeping Nathaniel so close to home is because of a young man named Jesus?"

Seth sighed, leaned his head back on her shoulder, and embraced her arms with his own. "That's not fair; we were supposed to work this out in the court." He smiled, stretched, and pulled her close.

"Seth, I also hear the rumors in the market. Women talk!" Yona sat down beside him. "I have heard about adultery and a virgin birth. I've heard things about gold and kings and angels. But they are just rumors." She reached over and took his hands. "I admit there is something about Jesus." She paused for a moment, staring at the flame flickering in the clay oil lamp on the table. "I can't put my finger on something, but he is one of the kindest, most considerate young men we know," Yona said, leaning in intently. She reached out and touched his face. "Seth, you are the wisest man I have ever known. You live a life that pleases God, and nothing pleases him more than loving your neighbor, regardless of what people might say."

After a long silence, Seth finally sighed as if he realized what he needed to do. "You are a gift from God." He stood up, placed his hands on each side of Yona's long black hair, and kissed the top of her head. "I am a better man and father because of you."

She put her hand on his and smiled. "Go now. Go talk to our son."

Seth entered their woodshop and found Nathaniel sitting in a chair in front of the small fire pit, poking the coals with a stick. Seth walked over and opened the woodshop shutters. He grabbed another stick and sat beside his son, poking at the coals in silence. Nathaniel sighed under his breath and prepared himself for another speech.

Seth told him, "We need to talk, son. But I'm going to do most of the talking. First, I need to apologize to you." Nathaniel lay his stick down, and he slowly slouched back in his chair a little. "Son, sometimes, we want our children to be so much more than we are, we just lose sight of the original goal. Sometimes, you just have to stop and take a look at what you're trying to do and make sure you're still on the right path to get there. I've held you to a high mark in learning and everything you do."

"But, Father—"

"Please, son, let me finish. Today is the day that I've had to stop and look at what I'm trying to accomplish. So stand up."

His father's confession caught Nathaniel off guard. "What?"

"Stand up, and let me take a look!"

This embarrassed Nathaniel a little, but he stood up, somewhat unsure of himself and where his father was going with this. By this time, Yona was standing in the open woodshop door watching her husband, but not in Nathaniel's line of sight.

"Let me tell you what I see." Seth took Nathaniel's hands and began to examine them. "I see a skilled craftsman who has a gift. And his ability has surpassed his teacher's." He walked around his son, looking him up and down, and continued. "I see a skilled businessman who is honest and responsible with everything God has given him." By this time, Nathaniel had tears streaming down his cheeks because of the much-needed validation from his father.

At that point, Yona walked into the room. Seth fought back his own emotions when she offered him a cup of oil to anoint his son and pronounce the Father's blessing. Slowly, he took the cup, poured the oil over his son's head, and began. "'May the Lord bless you and keep you; may the Lord make his face to shine upon you, and be gracious to you; may the Lord lift up his countenance upon you, and give you peace; may the Lord make your name great and curse those that curse you; and may your gifts be exalted and your family be blessed because of you. Amen'"

Nathaniel hugged his father and then his mother. "Thank you, Father. Thank you!"

"Now, go see your friends, and tell Jesus we said, 'Shalom,'" Seth responded.

Nathaniel walked backward and almost tripped over a small table. "Yes, Father, I will. Thank you!" He caught his balance, turned, and went out the door. Then, he waved and yelled, "Thank you!" again when he saw his parents standing in the window as he ran out the gate.

★★★

It was hot in Nazareth, but there was a gentle breeze, just enough to make it pleasant but not enough to kick up dust. When Nathaniel entered the gate at Jesus's house, Mary greeted him. "Good morning, Nathaniel. How are you today?"

"I'm well, thank you."

Mary lifted a waterpot to take it up the stairs to the roof, and Nathaniel quickly took it from her and followed her. "Just set it in the corner. Thank you," she said. Nearly everyone had a garden by their home, and Mary had just picked some herbs from hers and lay them out on the roof to dry.

"Hey, Nathaniel." Joseph reached the top of the stairs with

more herbs. "I think Jesus is out in the shop, possibly working on a shelf for these spices."

"It better be a big shelf, Joseph," Nathaniel said. "That's quite a harvest you have there!"

"Yes, it is. God is good," Joseph mumbled, trying to sort through the large variety of plants.

Nathaniel quickly got down the stairs and ran across the courtyard to the carpentry shop. Jesus saw Nathaniel coming and felt excited to see his friend.

"Hey, Nathaniel!" Jesus said, looking up from his work on the shelf. "Come help me. Your timing is great, and this is the part you're really good at."

"Let me see." Nathaniel ran his hands over the wood and checked out all the joints. "Nice job. It looks great." He helped Jesus attach the last shelf to the bottom, and Jesus made his mark on the bottom near the corner.

"Make yours too," Jesus said. "We did this together." Nathaniel agreed and put his mark in the corner by Jesus's. Jesus paused and rubbed his hand over Nathaniel's chiseled impression in the wood. "One day, your mark will be on something that will change the world."

Nathaniel laughed. "I hope so. Come on; your mother will cherish this. She has so many herbs."

Jesus looked up and smiled. "Yes, she does. Let's put it on the roof, and we can go to the market."

When they finished setting up the shelf, Nathaniel and Jesus walked out the gate and could see people stirring up dust at the end of the street. A number of visitors were in town that day. A caravan was outside of town, and lots of people were looking for supplies. Even a small caravan could double the number of people in the little town of Nazareth. It didn't really have much of a market compared to some of the bigger cities. Mainly, locals would lay out mats for extras from their gardens. People could see a variety of grapes, dates, figs, and vegetables.

Nathaniel and Jesus spent the day in the market talking with neighbors and even went out and walked through the caravan. There wasn't much to see except for some trade girls. Jesus encouraged Nathaniel to avoid even going in their direction, and they headed back into town.

As they walked past a vineyard on the edge of town, an elderly man wearing fine linen walked out onto the road toward them. He was short and had a quick step for an older man. "Nathaniel, is that you?"

Nathaniel approached the older man and embraced him. "Hello, Lemuel! Lemuel, meet my friend, Jesus."

"Hello, Jesus. Shalom. It's good to meet you." He took Jesus's hand, pulled him close, and kissed him on the forehead.

Jesus responded, "Shalom! What a wonderful vineyard."

"Oh, thank you, thank you. The Lord has blessed me and all I've set my hand to." Lemuel raised his hands and looked up toward the sky as he spoke. He seemed full of joy and moved quickly with a sense of purpose. "Come, come, come!" he said. Jesus and Nathaniel looked at each other and laughed as Lemuel grabbed their hands and pulled them down a path between the rows of grapes. He brought them to a large wooden awning that was so thick with grapevines that none of the afternoon sun could penetrate it.

"Please, please, help yourself." He motioned toward the huge clusters of grapes hanging down, some close to their faces. "I will get us something to drink." He walked over to a large orange clay pot and began to pour wine into cups from a ladle. "Here we are." Lemuel set the wine on a small table that sat low to the ground.

"Here now, Jesus, don't be so polite. It will take you all day picking those one at a time. Grab a cluster. Grab a cluster before they go bad!" Lemuel laughed out loud. Jesus looked at Nathaniel, shrugged his shoulders, pulled off a giant cluster, and brought it into the shade.

"Thank you, Lemuel," Jesus responded and laid the grapes

on the table. Red and blue cushions lay on the ground all around it. The gentle wind working its way through the vines made this place a cool retreat on a hot afternoon. Lemuel walked between them, stooped over like an old man, raised both his hands chest-high, and grunted, "Hm!" He looked at the ground. Neither Jesus nor Nathaniel knew what was going on. Lemuel stood up straight and looked back and forth between the two of them in surprise. And then he hunched back down like an old man and raised his hands. But this time, he looked up at the vines above his head and said, "Lord, please convince one or both of these strong young men to help an old man to the ground. Amen." Lemuel smiled, and Jesus and Nathaniel began to laugh.

"Oh, sorry." They both took an arm and slowly helped him down to the cushions.

"Ah." Lemuel lay all the way back with his hands above his head. "Thank you, Lord, for a nice rest for these old bones." Both boys laughed while enjoying the grapes. "Hand me my wine, Nathaniel." Lemuel sat up quickly and took a small cluster of grapes.

"I don't think you're in quite as bad a shape as you make out." Nathaniel poked at the older man.

"Maybe not …," Lemuel stammered, swallowing a mouthful of grapes. "However …" The old man paused, threw a grape straight up, and caught it in his mouth. He turned and winked at the boys. "However, I'll take as much help as I can get." Jesus and Nathaniel laughed and shook their heads. They spent the next few hours relaxing and talking about their families.

"So, where have you been, Lemuel?" Nathaniel asked.

"Well, I've been checking on my businesses here and there, and I've been gone far too long. I almost didn't make this harvest. But even if I hadn't, Ajeet would have taken care of it." Lemuel paused for a moment, leaned back on the cushions, and thoughtfully gazed out over the vineyard. He took a drink of his wine and continued. "But as it turns out, my return was a timely blessing from the Lord." He raised his eyebrows and smiled when he looked back at the boys. "You see, I met a rich jar vendor in the caravan, and he has decided that it's time to go into the wine-making business. I gave him my recipe and directions, and he bought almost every grape you can see."

"That's wonderful!" Nathaniel congratulated him.

"As a matter of fact, I've been hiring men all day and just hired the last group before you arrived."

Suddenly, a horn blew, and the workers began to bring in all the baskets full of grapes toward the front gate. "Don't stack them. Put each basket on the ground, and line up for your wages. Don't stack the baskets!" A middle-aged dark-skinned man gave directions and walked toward the awning.

"Hello, Ajeet!" Nathaniel walked out and greeted Lemuel's steward.

Ajeet's face softened when he smiled. He greeted Nathaniel and waved at Jesus. Then, he turned around, and his demeanor changed. "Line up for your wages. Make a line for your wages."

Ajeet and three other men brought out a table, a wooden box, and a chair. Two of the men had swords on their belt, and they stood on each side of Lemuel, who now sat in the chair behind the table. Ajeet opened the box and positioned it in front of his master.

"Approach the table one at a time, and do not crowd around the table," one of the men with a sword commanded. Each man received a denarius for a day's work, and each exited the gate.

"Thank you," one of the workers said as he took his wage.

"You're welcome. Thank you for working so hard," Lemuel responded.

The next man in line shouted when he received his wage, "Hey, what's going on here?" The two men on either side of Lemuel took a step forward with a hand on their sword. Lemuel raised his hand, and they both stood their ground.

Lemuel spoke in a calm voice and slowly stood up to speak to the worker. "What seems to be distressing you, my friend?"

The worker opened his hand and moved closer to Lemuel. "Those men worked one hour, and you also paid them a denarius." Suddenly, both his guards drew their swords and moved toward the man. Both their blades pointed toward the man at waist level.

"Did I not promise you a denarius this morning, when we made our agreement? Did I not?" Lemuel raised his voice and spoke to the remaining workers in line. "Can I not do what I want with what is mine?" He now shouted as he slammed the lid on the money box and looked into the eyes of the angry worker. "Or has your eye become evil because I am generous?" The angry man spat on the ground and grunted as he took his money and walked out the gate.

Lemuel waved his hand. "Ajeet." His servant took his spot and paid the rest of the men without incident. Then they arranged all the baskets and built a fire on the ground near them. The servants would stay all night and guard the grapes until the buyer came to get them in the morning.

"I'm sorry you had to see that. I do not lose my temper easily."

"I was glad to see it," Jesus remarked. "There is a valuable lesson to be learned in it all."

"Maybe so, but it's getting dark. Take one basket each to your families with my blessing, and go quickly. You don't want to be out on the streets after dark." Lemuel hurried them toward the gate.

"Thank you, thank you." They struggled with the baskets as they ran through the gate onto the road.

"Tell your father to come see me, Nathaniel. Yours too, Jesus. I think I may know him also." Lemuel yelled louder as they walked farther away. Jesus looked over his shoulder and struggled to wave and carry the basket. Jesus smiled as they started to run.

Lemuel did know his father, and his father knew him.

CHAPTER 6

M ary stood in the shade near the stable watching Jesus work. Several years had gone by, and he had stayed in Nazareth working as a carpenter. She watched him smoothing out several boards for a cart he was making for a vendor in Sepphoris. Many carpenters lived in Sepphoris, but the city was growing so fast it remained easy for Nathaniel and Jesus to go back and forth and find work to make a living.

Carpentry was hard work, and Jesus was a good carpenter, but his greatest offering came when he began to teach in the synagogue and at others' houses. People would sit listening to him for hours and walk away with a new understanding of life. He spoke about God as if he knew him personally and brought the law to life in a way words can't explain. Mary could feel a pull on his heart in a way only a mother could. He was being pulled away from carpentry and Nazareth. He was being pulled to a higher calling. He was being pulled toward his destiny.

"Here, son, take some water." Mary brought him a large pitcher of water and a cup. He was drenched in sweat, and Mary was glad he had removed his tunic and hung it on a wooden peg protruding from the plaster wall beside him.

"Ah, Mother, you're like an angel!" Jesus laughed and reached out to hug her.

"Don't you dare," she scolded him. "You're soaking wet."

He laughed again and said, "You can keep that." He took the

water pitcher and left her with the cup. First, he took a large gulp of water from the side of the pitcher. Then he turned his face toward the sky and slowly poured all the water over his face and hair. He smiled when he looked at his mother.

"Son." Mary warned him with her tone and her expression.

"Mother," Jesus responded, and she knew what he was about to do.

"Don't do—" But it was too late. He began to shake his head back and forth, slinging water all over her. Mary just stood there and took it. She started laughing.

"Why do you do this to me!" she playfully shouted and tried to block most of the water coming at her face. Jesus hugged her, and she protested. "Son, you're soaking wet!" Jesus laughed and ran up the stairs to the roof, Mary right behind him. He sat on a bench against the wall facing the countryside, and Mary sat down beside him and jokingly slapped his arm.

"It's a hot day, Mother. All I did is cool you off." She slapped his arm again and leaned into him.

"You're missing Father again. I miss him too." Jesus pulled his mother close and put his arm around her. Joseph had gotten sick and died about a year earlier. It happened very quickly; they didn't even have time to travel and get a doctor.

"I do miss him. He was a good man."

"Yes, and a good father," Jesus replied. They sat for a while in silence, looking out over the countryside.

"Mother, I know you have questions. Ask them," Jesus said. Then came a long pause.

Mary asked quietly, "Could you have … healed him?"

"Mother, the real question is 'Was I supposed to heal him?' And the answer is that I cannot do anything like that outside the will of my Father in heaven. You see, every man has a specific amount of time on this earth, and when believers die, it is no accident. Their time is complete on this earth, and they go to a better place. This is a difficult thing to understand because of the pain we feel. When a fisherman casts his net and brings up his fish, he has the power of life and death in his hands. He can release his fish and let it live, and his family will go hungry. Then he cannot make a living. If he keeps the fish, the fish must die. The fish must die because there is a greater purpose. It is impossible for man to understand the plans of God and why he does what he does. But know this: there is a greater purpose."

"Hello?" Nathaniel interrupted.

"I'm up here, Nathaniel. Coming down," Jesus said. "We are going to catch that ewe that's been hanging around back behind the garden." Jesus got up and kissed his mother.

"I love you, son. Thank you."

"I love you too, Mother."

Jesus asked Nathaniel as he went down the stairs. "You ready?"

Nathaniel sat at the bottom of the stairs, retying his sandals. "Let's go. I saw her back there just now. She's been back there for weeks."

Jesus picked up a shepherd's crook and they walked out of the gate together.

"Did you see Sera today?" Jesus asked.

How is it you always know where I've been and what I've been doing?" Nathaniel shook his head as they walked out into the brush.

"Well, first of all, I know you well. Second, you've loved her as long as I've known you. So what did her father say?"

Nathaniel just shook his head. "See, that's what I mean! How could you possibly know that?"

"There the ewe is," Jesus said quietly. "Remember, I've got the head, and you stay even with her shoulder, and don't get behind her; she will just run."

"Got it. She's up against the garden fence in perfect position," Nathaniel whispered.

Jesus slowly approached the ewe's head, and Nathaniel slowly made his way to her side. She jumped backward a bit, and

Nathaniel overcorrected and got behind her. She took off between them, running back behind some houses, and then turned and ran away from town.

"She's headed to the ravine. Come on; she will get trapped!" Nathaniel yelled, and they both ran after her. As they caught up to her, they both could see Nathaniel was right. She ran down into the narrow ravine, and she had only two ways out because the walls were too steep elsewhere.

"I'll go to the far end and wait, and then you bring her toward me. She's tired; she's not going anywhere." Nathaniel took the shepherd's crook from Jesus and climbed the steep embankment to make his way to the other end. Jesus was about to ease down into the ravine when he heard Nathaniel call out for him: "Jesus! Jesus!" He could hear panic in his friend's voice. He quickly climbed the hill and ran to find his friend.

As Jesus approached the other end of the ravine, he could see Nathaniel had slipped on the rocks and fallen face-first onto the bottom of the ravine. Nathaniel lay perfectly still, not because of his injuries but because his fall had disturbed a den of black vipers, the deadliest snakes in all of Judea. Jesus surveyed the situation and saw three of the vipers coiled up within striking distance of his friend's face.

"Do something!" The vibration of Nathaniel's voice caused one of the snakes to strike. Nathaniel lowered his head, and its fangs momentarily got caught in the top of his tunic before it retreated to its original position.

"Nathaniel, do not move, and do not speak. You will have to trust me," Jesus said.

Nathaniel lay there, perfectly still, and could hear Jesus walking up behind him. He assumed Jesus had picked up the shepherd's crook. He thought Jesus was ready to move and would hit the vipers. Instead, Jesus began to speak. "He who dwells in the secret place of the Most High will abide in the shadow of the

Almighty. I will say of the Lord, he is my refuge and my fortress, My God. In him I will trust" (Psalm 91:1–7 NKJV).

As Jesus got closer, the vipers got more and more agitated, and their bodies rose up higher in a striking position. Nathaniel still had his head down, but Jesus could hear him whisper, "What are you doing? Do something!"

Jesus continued. "Surely, he will deliver you from the snare of the fowler and from the perilous pestilence. He will cover you with his feathers, and under his wings you will take refuge; his truth will be your shield and buckler" (Psalm 91:1–7 NKJV).

"Jesus, please!" Nathaniel dared not move, and he could barely whisper.

Jesus kept speaking. "You will not be afraid of the terror by night, or of the arrow that flies by day, or of the pestilence that walks in darkness" (Psalm 91:1–7 NKJV).

The black vipers began to stir on the ground. Nathaniel almost threw up, thinking he was about to die an agonizing death, when Jesus finished speaking. "Of the destruction that lays waste at noonday, a thousand may fall at your side, and ten thousand at your right hand; but it shall not come near you" (Psalm 91:1–7 NKJV).

He spoke the final words more loudly and with authority, and the black vipers turned and retreated into their den. Jesus helped Nathaniel, weak and dripping with sweat, to his knees. "Come on. Let's get out of this ravine." He pulled Nathaniel to his feet and gave him the shepherd's crook to steady himself.

"I can't believe what just happened. I'm about to die a sure death, and you quote King David to the snakes," Nathaniel said.

After walking a short distance, Nathaniel stopped, leaned over, and put his hands on his knees. Jesus just sat down and let him get it all out. "You didn't get a stick or the shepherd's crook to save me! " Nathaniel began to raise his voice and flail his arms, yelling up at the sky. "You didn't get a rock to crush them. No, your first thought was to *quote the Psalms* to the black vipers!"

"And they left," Jesus added.

"Of course, they left!" Nathaniel yelled. "You practically quoted the whole book of Psalms to them!"

"Oh, come on. You're fine. Let's go." Jesus got up, smiling at Nathaniel's hysterics, and walked back toward town.

"You preached to the black vipers that were about to kill me ... *preached* to them!" Nathaniel stomped his feet and pulled and beat his tunic to get the dust out of it. "And he said *yes*! Her father said yes!"

Nathaniel talked to himself under his breath while he continued to beat the dust out of his clothes. "For the life of me, I'll never know how he knows these things."

Nathaniel carried on for a little longer and then settled down once they reached the narrow streets of Nazareth. When they rounded the corner toward Jesus's house, they were met by eight Roman soldiers and their centurion. They were escorting a prisoner in a wagon. He was reaching through the bars and cursing and spitting on people. Jesus and Nathaniel watched as they passed by, getting closer and closer to the prisoner. He had brown teeth and was filthy and stunk of urine and feces.

The prison wagon stopped right in front of them while a man moved his cart out of the street. They were at arm's length from the cart, and Nathaniel jumped when the prisoner slammed himself against the bars beside him. "I know who your friend is. I know who he is," the prisoner said in a high voice, and the stench of his breath made Nathaniel gag. The prisoner rolled on the floor, pulling his hair and laughing, repeating the same phrase over and over.

Suddenly, the convoy began to move again. "I know who you are. I know who you are, Jesus of Nazareth."

"Shut up." A soldier slammed his shield against the bars and knocked the prisoner back across the wagon. He got up and rushed toward the back of the wagon with blood now pouring from his nose. "I know who you are. I know who you are!" he screamed over and over until they were out of sight.

Nathaniel just stared at Jesus. He had a confused look on his face. "How could he possibly know your name? There's no way. How does he know?"

"Come on. Half of Jerusalem knows my name after the way you were yelling back there. Let's go."

Neither said a word walking home. Nathaniel was confused and didn't know what to think about the events of the afternoon. He was drained and hungry and decided not to think about it for now.

Chapter 7

Early in the morning, Jesus had three new carts lined up in the courtyard by his stable. The business owner from Sepphoris had arrived a short time before. The owner had three oxen and three extra men on horseback and they were eager to get back on the road. Mary opened the gate for them, and the men began to hitch one of the oxen to each cart.

"Well, Jesus, it looks like you received all the materials."

"I did, Greitus. Thank you. I also have some left over, if you want to take it back with you." Jesus motioned toward the neatly stacked lumber behind the carts.

"You keep that. I'm sure you will use it before I do. I don't know how you do it." Greitus ran his hand over the smooth wood of one of the carts. "It would take an average man twice as long to make carts of this quality." He walked over and handed Jesus a leather bag of coins.

"Thank you," Jesus responded. "I'll be gone for a while, but I thank you for your business." Jesus walked him back to his horse.

"That's a shame. It will be difficult to find another man who makes carts like these."

"Maybe not. Try my friend Nathaniel—last house on the left as you're leaving the city."

"I'll do that. Thanks again. I'm sure God will bless whatever you do," Greitus cried out as he rode off.

Jesus smiled and waved. He closed the gate and handed the

bag of coins to his mother. "This should last quite a while." Jesus followed his mother to a shaded area of the courtyard, where she was just finishing a new outer robe on her loom. "Is that for me?" he asked her.

"Yes, it is. It's time you had a new one. That one is getting a little worn." She referred to the robe he was wearing.

"But, Mother, didn't God tell Samuel that he looks on the heart and not on our outer appearance?" Jesus joked with his mother.

"He did. Now, take that off, and try this on." Mary walked over and handed him the new robe. "Give me that one, and I'll cut it up for rags." Mary put it on a shelf in a small dark room, where they stored utensils and pots.

"I'm sure you know you are quoting scripture that I taught you, right?" Mary raised her eyebrows and glanced up at him while she straightened his clothing. Jesus stood up straight and raised his arms out to the side even with his shoulders while she made adjustments and tied his belt around his waist. "And the first thing Samuel told Jesse is that 'Man looks on the outer appearance,' and I could be wrong, but men are the ones you do business with on a regular basis, so I want you to look your best."

"Thank you, Mother. You are right, as usual." Jesus smiled and sat down. He took two figs from her basket and ate one. "I need to leave for a while." He put the other fig back in the basket and pulled out a larger one.

"Oh? Where are you going?" Mary asked while wrapping new yarn around a spindle.

"I need to fast and pray. I will go see John first and then go out into the desert for a while."

"You're not going to miss Nathaniel's wedding, are you?"

"No, of course not, but it's very important that I spend some time away." Jesus spoke with a serious tone Mary hadn't heard very often.

Mary stopped what she was doing. "Things are about to change, aren't they?"

"Yes. Yes, they are," Jesus responded.

Mary got up and sat beside him. "We will have to leave all of this behind, won't we?"

"Yes, we will. My Father in heaven sent me here for a reason. I can't explain it to you right now, but it won't be easy." Jesus took his mother's hands. "Some things are going to happen that will be difficult for you to understand at first, but you have to trust me. Can you do that?"

"You know I can. I'll be ready when you get back."

"Thank you, Mother." Jesus hugged her and began to gather his things. "I'll have John take care of the donkey, and then I'll come back and get you. If you need anything, go to Nathaniel."

Jesus loaded several sheepskin containers to carry water on the back of his donkey. Mary brought some cheese, figs, and dried fish for the first part of his journey and placed them in a basket on the donkey's back. He kissed his mother and led the animal down the street toward Nathaniel's house.

As Jesus approached the gate, he saw his friend just outside the shop working on a plow. "Hey!" Jesus said, throwing a fig toward Nathaniel, who turned and caught it just before it hit him.

"Hey, thanks!" Nathaniel mumbled after taking a large bite from the giant fruit. "Where are you going?" Nathaniel asked, wiping juice from his beard with his tunic.

"I'm going to see John and spend some time away in prayer. Watch over my mother while I'm gone."

Nathaniel splashed some water on his face and washed his hands. He walked over to open the gate and asked, "When will you be back?"

"I'm not sure. In several weeks. They came and picked up the carts this morning, so she'll be fine."

"You know, Sera and I will marry in a few weeks," Nathaniel reminded him.

"I'll be back in time," Jesus reassured him.

"You better be!" Nathaniel laughed. "I'll check in on your mother; don't worry."

"Thank you." The two men embraced, and Nathaniel watched Jesus walk down the road, leaving Nazareth. "Safe travels, my friend. Safe travels."

★★★

Jesus followed the Jordan River south and was two days' travel from his home when he saw a large gathering of people on the riverbank in the distance. Jesus smiled and hurried the donkey along, excited to see his cousin John. He tied the donkey to a tree and began to make his way to the water. John stood in the water with several of his disciples, and people lined up to get baptized. Jesus walked through the crowd, greeting strangers and meeting people from different towns and cities around the region.

While Jesus talked, he could hear John preaching with sincerity in a loud voice. "Repent. Repent, for the kingdom of God is here. Come, be baptized, and sin no more. I am here to testify of another coming after me. The one who's coming ..." John paused when he saw Jesus. "There's another one coming, one who I am ... unworthy to tie his sandals." John got quieter as Jesus approached, his disciples all stopped, and everyone watched Jesus walk into the water. Most people wondered why John had stopped preaching, but his disciples and those close around him could still hear him.

"Behold, the lamb of God who takes away the sins of the world." John could barely speak and looked unsteady because of the sudden revelation from God. He swayed a little, and Jesus grabbed John's arm to hold him up.

"It's okay, John," Jesus said and smiled.

John softly said to him, "It's you; you're the one. God just showed me that you're the one—the Messiah!" John braced himself by holding Jesus's shoulders and said, "I can't baptize you. You have to baptize me!"

"No, John, you have to do this to fulfill all that God has begun."

So John baptized him, and when he raised him up out of the water, Jesus took a deep breath as the Holy Spirit came down to him like a dove. At that same moment, a voice came down from heaven and said, "This is my Son that I love, and he brings me great joy!"

Jesus embraced John. "Thank you, John. It starts now. Everything changes now!" Jesus quietly said to John.

"Continue. I'll be back." John motioned to his disciples.

Together, the two of them walked out of the river and climbed up onto a large, flat rock. Jesus pulled off his new robe and laid it out to dry. John lay back on the rock with his eyes closed and asked, "How long have you known?"

"As long as I can remember," Jesus responded.

"I'm confused. This is all hard to believe."

"Satan is counting on that." Then, Jesus got up, squeezed the water out of his robe, and laid it out again.

"John, this will all get harder before it gets better. You are doing all of this for a very important reason. I need you to keep doing it. We have to stir the hearts of the people. We have to remove their blinders so they can see. It will seem small at first, but the kingdom of darkness knows we are here. Time is short, and there is much to do." Jesus stood up, put his robe back on, and tied his belt. "I need you to do this. We need you to do this … and I need you to endure until the end. Are you with me, John?"

John grabbed Jesus again by the shoulders, kissed him on each cheek, looked him in the eyes, and nodded in affirmation. He turned around, raised his arms as he slowly walked down the side of the hill, and began to yell again. "Repent. Repent, for the kingdom of God is at hand. We must turn away from our sins and worship the one true God. Repent. Repent, and be baptized in the name of the Lord."

Jesus walked back through the growing crowd toward his donkey. He gave his remaining food to one of the disciples and made arrangements for the care of the animal. He looked back at John, baptizing and preaching to the people, smiled, and walked away from the crowd to begin his time in the desert.

★★★

It had been weeks since Jesus left John and the crowds of people at the river. For days and days, Jesus walked and prayed. He didn't eat, but he did have his waterskins, and the Holy Spirit made sure he found different places to refill them.

On one hot, sunny day, he found a small cave. It felt nice to get out of the midday sun and have a place to sleep at night. Jesus could feel his time of prayer and fasting coming to an end. On the fortieth day, he was still asleep in the early morning. The sky began to take on a pink hue as the sun climbed up behind the mountains in the distance. He stirred a little and realized the sound of a fire and the aromas of fresh bread and cooking fish had awakened him. He rolled over, and there, just a few feet from the cave entrance, stood a tall, stout man dressed in fine white linen. His back was to Jesus, but he knew exactly who it was.

"Well, good morning. I'm making us some breakfast. You're probably hungry after thirty-nine days." The man began to laugh. "You'll be glad to know I actually just caught this fish with my net—you know, the whole 'life and death of a fish is in the hands of the fisherman' thing." He laughed mockingly, making fun of Jesus's words to his mother. Jesus walked around the fire and sat on a rock across from the man and just watched.

This was a bold appearance for his enemy, the devil. He knew Jesus was weak, and he wanted to know how weak he was in his humanity. So he set up a large, flat rock and built a large fire below it. Five rocks lay on top of the flat one, and when the devil moved them around with a stick, some would sizzle, and all the smells of cooking food got stronger.

"You know, there's a rumor going around that you're actually the Son of God!" Satan said loudly and laughed, mocking him once again. "If that's the case, why don't you just turn these stones into the real thing?" Satan stared at him and sneered, "Go ahead. Give it a try."

Jesus just looked at him, slowly stood up, gently took the stick from his hand, and said, "It is written, 'Man will not live only on bread but by every word that comes from the mouth of God.' When he spoke, he used the stick to raise the flat rock, and all the smaller rocks fell into the fire.

The evil one said, "So, we are going to stand on the words of the ever-almighty God, then? Fine! Let's do that very thing. Let's stand on them."

Jesus agreed to go with him, and they immediately stood on the highest part of the temple in Jerusalem. "So, let's stand, shall we? Let's stand on the Word of God in his holy city, on his holy temple. And please let me quote his … *Holy Word*." Satan bowed, waving his arms out by his sides. He spoke his every word with contempt, and every action was irreverent and arrogant. "It is written." He patted his chest and raised one hand while he cleared his throat. "It is written, 'He will put his angels in charge of keeping you safe, and in their very hands they will hold you up so you won't even hit your foot against a stone.' So jump."

Jesus, once again, just looked at him, completely unmoved by anything he said or did.

"If you're the Son of God, then jump! *Jump*, and show me it's true!" Satan drew close to Jesus and whispered in his ear, "Show me the Word of God is true. Show me … jump."

Jesus turned so they were eye to eye, and he quietly said, "It is written again. You will not tempt the Lord your God."

Then the devil took him higher, to the top of a mountain, and said, "Look. Look at all that is in this world. Look at the luxuries and the glorious riches in all these kingdoms. You know they all belong to me. However, I could give them to you if you will just bow down to me and call me Lord."

Jesus had had enough. "Satan! Leave this place now! It is also written, 'You must worship the Lord your God and serve him and only him.' When he said these words, the devil was gone. Immediately, the heavens opened up, and legions of angels surrounded the mountain. Several came down, bringing fresh water and food to meet all his needs.

CHAPTER 8

J esus returned to the region of Galilee, and on his way back to Nazareth, he taught in many of the surrounding synagogues. He was full of the power of the spirit, and people began to talk. His reputation began to grow throughout the area as a teacher who taught with authority and one who did miracles.

When he came to Nazareth, it was getting dark, and he could hear the celebration from outside the small town. Jesus smiled because he knew Nathaniel's wedding feast was well underway.

"Nathaniel, he'll be here. He said he would." Sera smiled and comforted her husband. "You know that if anyone will keep their word, it's Jesus."

"I know ... I know." Nathaniel half smiled.

Sera looked up and saw Jesus approaching from behind Nathaniel. She smiled and was about to tell her husband when Jesus motioned for her not to. Jesus came up behind him and covered Nathaniel's eyes with his hands. "Guess who?" Jesus said quietly with a big smile.

Everyone laughed, and a huge smile came across Nathaniel's face. "You made it!" Nathaniel exclaimed.

"I told you I would." Jesus embraced his friend and his new bride. "Congratulations to you both! Oh, I have something for you." He reached down into his bag and pulled out a pair of doves carved out of acacia wood.

"They are beautiful, Jesus! Thank you," Sera said, admiring the gift.

"Bring some wine. Let's celebrate!" Nathaniel shouted.

Jesus hugged his mother, who was there for the wedding. The festivities went on well into the night. The celebration went on for several days, and then life began to return to normal in the small town.

News had spread, even back to Nazareth, about Jesus and his reputation as a teacher, including some of the miracles. But rumors were just that—rumors.

The rabbi of the small synagogue in Nazareth asked Jesus to teach there. Jesus decided he would on the next Sabbath. On that day, the building filled with anticipation, and everyone was glad to see him. Even those people had heard of his reputation as a powerful teacher.

When the rabbi invited him up to speak, Jesus stood to read the scroll that was handed to him. Everyone was silent, and all eyes rested on him. Different readings are read on specific days of the year. Jesus found the appointed place in the scroll of Isaiah and began to read: "'The Spirit of the Lord is on me. He has anointed me to bring good news to the poor. He has sent me to proclaim that captives will be freed, that the blind will see, that the oppressed will be set free, and that the time of the Lord's favor is now'" (Luke 4:18–19 NKJV).

Jesus sat down beside Nathaniel and said, "The reading of this written passage is fulfilled today as I have read it."

The people were amazed at his words and asked if this wasn't the son of Joseph the carpenter. Jesus said, "I'm sure at one point, you will quote a proverb to me and say, 'Physician, go and heal yourself and perform the same miracles you do in Capernaum, but I know that a prophet won't be received in his own town.'"

Jesus paused and looked at the group of men sitting in the front and the women and children sitting in the back. "And you also know that Elijah was in Israel during the three-and-a-half-year drought, during the famine, and he wasn't sent to the Jewish widows but instead to a Gentile—Sarepta in Sidon?" The men began to stir a little and grumble when Jesus talked about the Lord blessing a Gentile instead of the Jews. "What's more—"

"Jesus! What are you doing?" Nathaniel said under his breath and nudged him.

"What's more, with all the lepers in Israel, God sent Elisha to heal another Gentile, Naaman the Syrian."

When Jesus said that, they were furious at the insult and the suggestion that he would take his teachings to the Gentiles. "Seize him!" they yelled.

Jesus turned to his friend. "Get Sera and my mother, and meet me at the edge of town by your house." In the chaos, Nathaniel easily moved to the back of the room and led both women to safety.

Some of the angry men tore their clothes and yelled, "Blasphemy! Seize him!" So the men grabbed Jesus and led him out of the building to the edge of a cliff outside of town. The men were about to throw him off, but in the chaos, they actually lost track of him. The Holy Spirit led Jesus through the middle of the crowd, and he made his way up the street toward Nathaniel's house.

"Jesus! What was that about? I'm surprised they didn't kill you," Nathaniel said.

"They tried," Jesus said as he closed the gate to Nathaniel's house.

"My father is really upset with you. What is going on? Jesus, what is going on? You had your mother sell your house and all your father's tools—*your* tools! What will you do now? Plus, what are Sera and I supposed to do? Everyone knows we are friends, and now, they hate us. Why did you say those things? Are you crazy? Have you lost all reason? I could have told—"

"Nathaniel, please!" Jesus said sternly to him for the first time in his life. "There is more going on here than you know."

"Well, then, please, please explain to me why the men of Nazareth just tried to kill you, and tell me why I will probably have to move out of town as well." Nathaniel raised his voice.

"Look, I'm sorry. I can't explain everything right now. We have to leave early in the morning. Where is my mother?" Jesus asked.

"She's on the roof. Father said you both can stay up there tonight."

"Thank you. We will leave in the morning before they wake up."

Jesus walked up the stairs and saw Mary sitting on a pile of straw. She was looking up at the stars, which were just becoming visible in the evening sky. "You know, son, it was a night like this when Gabriel appeared to me."

Mary smiled and looked up at her son. He gently smiled back, sat beside her, and said, "'You will conceive in your womb, and you will have a son, and you will name him Jesus. He will be called great and will be called the Son of the Most High. The Lord God will give him the throne of his father David. He will reign over the house of Jacob forever, and his kingdom will have no end.'"

Mary looked over at him. "How do you know that? I never told you that ... How?"

"Mother, I was there." Jesus looked up at the stars, and Mary suddenly felt afraid. There was more to this than the angel had told her, and it felt like just the beginning. Jesus pulled her close. "It's all right, Mother. Try to get some rest." But Mary knew it would be difficult to sleep tonight.

Jesus stayed up late into the night praying and smiled when he looked over and saw that his mother had fallen asleep. He quietly made his way down the stairs and out the gate to make preparations for their early-morning journey to Capernaum.

Several hours later, he woke Nathaniel and his mother. "Come. We must leave before the villagers wake up."

Nathaniel made arrangements for Sera to stay with his parents. She would stay safe there until he could come back for her. They quietly walked across the stone courtyard, out the gate, and onto the streets of Nazareth for the last time. Jesus had a small oil lamp. He led them with the light down the dirt road away from town, where they came upon a wooden cart hitched to an ox. Waterpots and a few baskets of food sat on the back of the cart, where a donkey was also tied.

Nathaniel took the lamp from Jesus and began to look through some of the things. "Where did you get all of this?" Nathaniel opened a wooden box and found Jesus's full set of carpenter's tools. "I thought you sold—"

"It's not important. We must leave now," Jesus said quietly and lifted Mary up onto the cart.

They took their time traveling to Capernaum and arrived that same afternoon. Capernaum, a fishing community, was about four times the size of Nazareth, and it had a much larger market and synagogue. The main street was busy with the buying and selling of fresh and dried fish. Unnoticed, Jesus, Nathaniel, and Mary worked their way through the crowd until they approached the synagogue.

"Teacher! Teacher!" The rabbi of the synagogue came running out to meet Jesus. "Teacher, you're back! It's so good to see you again." Jesus waved with a big smile and helped his mother down from the cart. "Please take the teacher's mother in so that she may refresh herself," the rabbi told two of the attendants, who led Mary up the steps and into the courtyard.

"Thank you, Rabbi." Jesus kissed him on each cheek as they embraced. "I have no better companion in the world than this man. Please meet my friend Nathaniel."

The rabbi embraced Nathaniel and kissed him on the forehead. "Any friend of Jesus is a friend of ours. Please come; let's go inside and refresh ourselves." The rabbi led the way, and the two men followed a few steps behind.

"I'm guessing you taught a different lesson here than you did in Nazareth," Nathaniel said sarcastically.

Jesus just smiled and shook his head. "Come on." He took Nathaniel by the back of the neck and playfully nudged him forward.

"Come sit down. You must be tired from your journey." The rabbi and elders sat down as Jesus sat on a cushion in the middle of the group of men. Mary had a pitcher of wine and was filling their glasses.

"Thank you, Mother." Jesus gestured toward her. Mary smiled, and several of the elders took note of the way Jesus showed gratitude and gentleness toward his mother. Most men, including holy men, assumed this was a duty rather than a kindness.

The rabbi said, "Jesus, from the looks of the belongings on your cart, it looks like you've come to stay, and if that's true, I would like you to stay with a man I know. He has a large home and has been here daily asking for you. You made quite an impression the last time you came here. God worked astounding miracles through you. Also, you're a very good teacher, and we all look forward to hearing you again soon."

"Thank you," Jesus responded. "Rabbi, Nathaniel is a man who works with his hands and is an excellent carpenter."

"Say no more. I know a boatbuilder who is in need of a man just like you." He motioned toward Nathaniel. "Tovias can take you to him now, if you're ready." Nathaniel said thank you and followed the man toward the gate. The rabbi called out to Tovias as they walked across the courtyard. "We will take Jesus and his mother to Gavriel's home. Take Nathaniel there when you're finished."

Jesus stood up and began to walk quickly toward the gate. "Thank you, Rabbi, but I need to go with Nathaniel. I have some men to meet."

As the rabbi motioned toward some of the elders, he said, "Oh, okay, we will take your mother and bring your things."

"Thank you," Jesus cried out and waved as he ran to catch up with Tovias and Nathaniel.

They walked toward the water and the small clay buildings that lined the road near the shore. Tovias began to walk slower as they approached an elderly man struggling to replace a plank in an older boat. He bent over slightly, and his hands contorted from the many years he had obviously worked on boats. Even as he struggled, he whistled and seemed to have a pleasant disposition.

Nathaniel looked over at Tovias and smiled and nodded. "Here, let me help you." Nathaniel stepped in and expertly began to fit and attach the board in place.

"Oh, thank you, thank you." The old seaman laughed as he moved over and patted Nathaniel on the back. "The Lord truly hears my prayers. These hands aren't what they once were, but my eyes and mind are as sharp as a bird of prey!" The old man looked at Nathaniel with a smile. He spoke with a soft, hoarse voice but had a gentle and kind disposition.

"I believe that." Tovias spoke up as he stepped toward his friend. "Amos, this is Nathaniel, and his friend Jesus."

"Well, hello, Tovias. Jesus, it's good to meet you." Amos reached out and embraced them both. "And Nathaniel, I can tell you are a fine carpenter."

"He's the best, and we have just moved here from Nazareth." Jesus stepped up and placed a hand on Amos's back. The older man carefully watched Nathaniel.

"Good, good," Amos quietly commented as Nathaniel finished the task. "Now, get the pitch, and seal it up." Nathaniel got the hot pot of pitch from the fire, and Amos carefully inspected the repair. "Nathaniel, when can you start?" Amos asked, moving out of his way.

"It looks like I already have." Nathaniel smiled, and they all laughed.

"Oh, the Lord is good, and his mercies endure forever!" Amos exclaimed as he took Jesus's hands and stepped back and forth as if he were dancing. Jesus laughed with joy at this man's faith and thankfulness.

"Amos, I wish I could stay, but I need to get back to the synagogue," said Tovias.

"Thank you, my friend. My heart is full and at peace." Amos kissed Tovias on each cheek and waved goodbye as his friend departed.

"I must be going too," Jesus said and embraced Amos. He looked at Nathaniel and said, "And I'll see you later."

Jesus left them to their work, walked along the beach, and prayed. Several people recognized him, and he began to teach until the crowd pressed in around him. When he noticed some men washing their nets, he got up, waded into the water, and got into one of their boats.

"Simon, that's the teacher I was telling you about. He has done many miracles. Just look at all the people. Come on." Andrew was excited. "Come on!" Andrew pulled the net and ran through the water. Simon just shook his head and followed him reluctantly. He was tired and had seen lots of false teachers get famous, never to be seen again.

"Come, Simon. Let me help you." Jesus reached down to help them both into the boat.

"How do you know my name?" Simon asked.

"Push out from the shore just a little," Jesus said. So they did and dropped an anchor just a little ways out. Jesus stood at the front of the boat and continued to teach the people for a short time. Andrew marveled at his teaching, and Simon listened half-heartedly, trying to stay awake.

Jesus finished, but the crowds stayed, waiting to see if he would resume teaching. "Simon, let's push out into the deep and catch some fish," Jesus said as he moved to the back of the boat and sat down.

"Master …" Simon started respectfully, but it was easy to tell Simon wanted to be anywhere but here. "We fished all night and caught nothing. We are fishermen. There are no fish out there today. However, I will do as you've asked." Simon pulled up the anchor, and they drifted slowly out to the deeper water. The other two men with them were near shore and raised their arms, questioning Simon's motivation for going back out.

"Stop here, and let down the net." Jesus intently looked at Simon. Simon nodded to Andrew, wondering why they had to go through this, but at the same time, he had a weary curiosity. He could only think of sleep, so he hoped that this would all be over quickly.

The sea was perfectly still, and the sounds from shore faded as the crowd of people left for their homes. There wasn't even a breeze. They sat there for several minutes. Andrew watched the water, and Simon leaned against the mast of the small boat and began to fall asleep.

Simon twitched and opened his eyes, realizing he had fallen asleep. His eyes burned and got heavy. He stared down at the net and was about to fall back asleep when the net jerked and pulled at both ends. Andrew was already pulling on one end. Simon slipped and fell trying to gather the other end. Jesus stood up, grabbed that end, and handed it to Simon as he recovered his balance. Jesus laughed, and Simon just looked at him, trying to make sense of it all. He pulled and pulled, but the weight was too great.

"Andrew, pull!" Simon shouted. Simon looked at Jesus, and they both laughed. The harder they pulled, the more the small boat sunk down into the water. "James! John, come help!" Simon shouted back toward the shore.

By this time, the net had begun to tear in one spot. Andrew quickly tied a rope to it and secured it to the boat. "James, grab this corner!" Andrew shouted when the other two men arrived. "John, you help Simon." They secured the net to both boats and tried to quickly gather the mass of fish into the boats before the net tore open. Fish flew back and forth as each man quickly threw them into the boats.

83

Simon looked down and saw that the boats were so full of fish that they were getting dangerously close to sinking. "Stop, no more." Simon went to Jesus on his knees. "Lord, I am a sinful man. You should leave. What business do you have with a man like me?" Simon's eyes began to water. He had never witnessed anything like this. The other men sat sweating and panting from the strenuous work.

"James, John, untie the net." They did as Jesus asked, and the weight on the net released as the fish swam free. Jesus pulled Simon to his feet from the flopping fish. "Simon, come and follow me, and I will make you all fishers of men."

Simon embraced Jesus for a moment and said, "All right, let's go. We will fish for *men*!" They all laughed and sat on the piles of fish, slowly rowing the overburdened boats back to shore.

Once again, crowds began to gather, and many men jumped into the water and helped pull the boats up onto shore. The people were all shocked by the men's catch, and they stood around, wondering how they would deal with all these fish. Jesus told them to get four large fish for dinner, and they began to walk with Jesus back toward Amos's shop. Simon turned around and yelled to the crowd, "Free fish for everyone!" All the people went crazy, and there was plenty of fish for all who were there.

Jesus smiled. "Come, Simon, son of Jonas. I'm going to call you Peter."

They stopped back by Amos's and gave Amos a large fish. Nathaniel was just finishing up, and it was late in the day. Jesus introduced everyone and got directions from Amos's to Gavriel's home. They took a path along the beach, and Simon told Nathaniel about their unbelievable story.

The walk to Gavriel's home was a short one. When they approached the gate, they heard someone call out, "Teacher, please come in." A very short man dressed in fine linen ran and opened the gate. "Teacher, it is so good to see you. Please, sit down." Shaking Jesus's hand, he said, "Hello, I am Gavriel. Welcome to my home." He kissed Jesus and warmly greeted each of the other men.

Gavriel had many hired servants. Two of them took the fish, and several came with washbasins, clean water, and towels. Gavriel bowed down, removed Jesus's sandals, and washed his feet. The servants did the same for Nathaniel and all Jesus's new disciples.

"Gavriel, thank you for your generosity," Jesus said and introduced them all. This is Peter, James, John, and Peter's brother, Andrew. And this is my good friend Nathaniel."

"Thank you Rabbi." I would like you all to stay with me. We have plenty of rooms, the weather has been nice, and the roof is very large and open. It so big you could all sleep up there." Gavriel laughed.

"That would be nice. Thank you," Jesus responded.

"We have plenty of wine and fruit on the roof, if you would like to relax while dinner is prepared. Jesus, I believe your mother is up there. She and I had a good talk." Gavriel chuckled as he motioned them toward the stairs.

Jesus followed the disciples and the servants. Right before he got to the stairs, Gavriel asked him a question. "Rabbi, my nephew is getting married in two days in Cana. Would you do me the honor of attending and bringing your disciples? Your mother and Nathaniel are also welcome, of course. I would like for you to sit at my table. We could travel to Cana and then go from there to Jerusalem for Passover."

"Gavriel, I would enjoy that very much. Thank you," Jesus replied.

Gavriel leaned in Jesus's direction. "We will leave tomorrow in the cool of the day. I will take care of everything. Thank you, Rabbi. This will make my family very happy." He patted Jesus on the back and followed him up the stairs.

Gavriel was a wonderful host, and he kept everyone laughing for most of the evening. Jesus sat back and enjoyed the moment. Everyone was smiling and happy. No one had a care in the world that night. These men had no awareness of what they were about to experience. And for the time being, that was okay.

CHAPTER 9

The next morning, Gavriel had a caravan waiting outside when everyone woke up. It had several camels and donkeys, plus two carts with supplies for the wedding. They traveled for half the day and only stopped to eat and rest. Gavriel was a rare man. He was rich, generous, funny, and pleasant to be around. He and Nathaniel quickly became good friends on the trip. Gavriel loved good woodwork and wanted to learn more about the trade.

It was early afternoon when they arrived in Cana, and wedding preparations were underway. They all rested in a large covered area, snacking on grapes and cheese so as not to spoil their appetite for the festivities. This evening would serve several fatted calves along with many delicious platters of fruits and cakes.

Jesus walked down a hill and stood under some trees with Nathaniel and the disciples. A few guests were there, and Jesus began to teach them. This time, Peter listened closely with great interest. Some fishermen might have looked at the event in the boats as a lucky catch. Peter knew it was much more and was eager to learn more from Jesus. His teachings were all about love. He taught in a different way. People actually felt as if he loved them. This was strange to Peter, but something he could get used to.

Nathaniel looked at Peter and wondered why Jesus would choose uneducated fishermen as disciples. But at this point, nothing Jesus did surprised him.

"Everyone, please come. Let's begin," Gavriel called out from up the hill. They all made their way back to the house and sat down at the decorated tables spread all around the grounds. Musicians began to play, and wine was served. There were several seating areas, and so many people attended some had to stand.

"Jesus! Over here." Gavriel called their group over to one of the three head tables toward the front. "Here. Please sit here." He pulled a chair out for Jesus. "And here are seats for all of you." He motioned to Mary, Nathaniel, and the disciples. They all sat down, and a servant brought wine and platters with bread, cheese, and an assortment of delicious fruits.

Everyone was having a wonderful time when the music stopped. The crowd got quiet, and suddenly, the bride and groom appeared, and they all began to shout and cheer. At that point, the celebration really got underway. They had a wonderful evening, and everything went as planned.

Gavriel stood up and excused himself to congratulate his nephew and his bride. Before he left, he took his napkin, folded it and refolded it several times, and laid it on his chair. Everyone looked at him, and he slowly looked up and said, "As you all know, folding your napkin is a sign that you're coming back. And yet, you are looking at me like I am a crazy man." Gavriel looked inquisitively at each of them with a sly grin.

"It's not that you fold it as much as how many times you fold it. And then you sit on it. You've done it *several* times!" Nathaniel felt embarrassed, and everyone around him laughed. The music had stopped in the middle of his sentence, and he unexpectedly shouted for no reason.

As the laughter died down, Gavriel refolded his napkin, neatly set it in the middle of his chair, and sat on it. He leaned forward and began to tell his tale. Everyone looked around, smiling, knowing he would tell a good story. "Now, there was a king in a faraway land, from the land of …" He stopped and thought for a moment. "Oh, yes, the land of Pernomesia. Yes, the land of Pernomesia." Everyone laughed at the made-up name.

He continued. "In the land, there was a king, and he only had one son. He was a powerful and just ruler. He was respected throughout the land." Gavriel lowered his voice and leaned in. "You see, King ... um ..." He looked around, puzzled. "Oh, yes, King Pilmert!"

"Pilmert? That's a horrible name!" Nathaniel laughed with everyone else.

Gavriel grinned and continued. "As I was saying, King Pilmert was a tall man and stood over everyone in the kingdom, as did his father and his father's father. The problem was his son—we will call him Gavy—was a young man of short stature, and none of the servants would listen to him. You see, they had come to relate authority with a tall stature."

"Oh, a short man named Gavy, like Gavriel." Nathaniel playfully mocked him.

Gavriel chuckled and pointed in Nathaniel's direction. "That's enough out of you!" Everyone laughed again, waiting patiently for the story. Gavriel continued. "Now, the king was perplexed. He would leave his son to rule one day, and he had to somehow gain the servants' respect for him. So, he called in his most trusted advisor, whose name was ... um ... Nathaniel. His name was Nathaniel!"

Nathaniel spoke up. "That's more like it!" Peter and the disciples just shook their heads and laughed.

Gavriel said, "Anyway, the king called Nathaniel in and told him about the problem. The king's advisor thought for a moment and then came up with a plan. So the next day, the servants went into the throne room and noticed the young prince sitting high on his chair, and they showed him the highest level of respect from that day forward." Gavriel got up and started to walk away.

"Hey, wait, what was the plan? Wait, what ... Gavriel?" they shouted. "Come back."

Gavriel spun around, winked, and walked back to the table. "All right, now you see," Gavriel said. Jesus smiled as Gavriel continued his story. Several guests who knew him had gathered around to hear the storyteller. "The young prince would sit on his throne next to his father, and behind them were silk curtains of various colors. So the brilliant advisor would go in and pull the bottoms of the curtains up onto his chair and fold them over many times. Then, the young prince would come in before the servants and sit high on the throne so he might be respected. And so I fold my napkin the same way, and it has worked the same for me ever since."

The table and surrounding guests started to laugh, but only because Gavriel laughed so hard and thought it was so funny.

"Terrible story!" Nathaniel poked fun at him.

Mary had excused herself before Gavriel began and was walking up to the table as the laughter began to die down. All the other guests had sat back down, and Gavriel had left to see his nephew. Mary said, "Son, we need your help. Gavriel's brother has run out of wine."

Jesus looked up at her. "Mother, why have you brought this to me?"

Mary leaned in closer to Jesus and said, "You're the only one here who can do anything about this. You can see how many people showed up."

Nathaniel and the disciples watched intently, wondering why she was telling him.

Jesus lowered his voice a little. "Mother, it is not time yet."

Mary turned to several servants standing close by and said, "Whatever he tells you to do, then do it." They bowed, acknowledging her authority, and they looked at Jesus. He looked around the table, all eyes on him.

Jesus motioned for the servants to come closer. "Get all your waterpots, and fill them full of water—all of them." They bowed with respect, left, and then returned a short time later.

"We have done what you said," the head servant reported.

"Now, pour some out, and give it to your master." Jesus

and the group at the table watched as the servant took water to the master of the feast. He drank it and then complimented the bridegroom on saving the good wine until last.

Nathaniel and the disciples just looked at Jesus. He motioned to the servants to bring some to the table, and they poured it for them and placed the container on the table. Slowly, they all began to sip the water, but it wasn't water.

Andrew looked at Peter and smiled. "I told you!" he whispered.

Nathaniel looked inside his cup and took a drink. He pulled the cup back quickly and looked at Jesus. He smiled, and he watched the disciples. Nathaniel slowly took another sip, placed his cup on the table, and turned to Jesus. "I saw them put water into those pots. And then they drew wine from the same exact pot. What did you do? How did you—?"

"Jesus, come meet my nephew," Gavriel called and waved from a few tables away.

Jesus patted Nathaniel's forearm as he stood up and said, "God is good, my friend," and he walked away. Nathaniel took his cup, stood up, and walked over to the waterpots. He tasted the wine in each one and looked at the servants. They just shrugged their shoulders in amazement. Nathaniel sat down on a large stone and watched the disciples excitedly talking back and forth.

Andrew looked over at him and raised his cup. "Can you believe it?"

Nathaniel couldn't hear Andrew because the music had started back up, but he could make out what he said. He raised his cup and forced a smile in response. He sat there alone on the stone and just stared at his cup, bewildered. "No, no, I can't believe it," Nathaniel said quietly to himself. He raised his hand to wipe his face with a napkin he had picked up from the table. Bringing it up to his face, he noticed it was folded very neatly, and as he looked over at the table, he realized he had not picked up his napkin but Jesus's folded napkin. He smiled, thinking about Gavriel's story, and just shook his head, not understanding how Jesus had turned water into wine.

Gavriel had made arrangements for all of them to stay the night and then leave early the next morning for Jerusalem. It would take about five days to get from Capernaum to Jerusalem, but because they were in Cana, they only had a three-day journey.

Jesus remembered that Joseph had brought his mother and him to Jerusalem for Passover every year from his early childhood. Since then, Jesus and his mother had continued to travel with friends and neighbors yearly since Joseph's death.

As they all approached from a distance, a haze lay over the city from the dust all the people stirred up coming in for Passover. Jerusalem had about one hundred thousand people living in the area, but that would swell to nearly four million during Passover. The crowds were almost unbearable. Even though this was a holy time, Passover would also attract some of the worst humanity had to offer. The huge blend of Jews and Gentiles was always on the edge of getting out of control.

Rome had had control of Jerusalem and the surrounding area for nearly ninety years, and the Jewish people hated it more every year. The Roman presence always grew tenfold during Passover, which made things worse. There was usually some underground revolt brewing, and the Roman soldiers were especially cruel during the holiday to prevent any rebellion. When they saw soldiers, it was best to avoid them and walk the other way.

It took quite awhile for the group to make their way through the crowded streets to Gavriel's brother's home. As they entered the gates of the large home, many servants came to take care of the animals and unload their things. Gavriel motioned toward a man identical in appearance to himself, "Jesus, meet my brother, Lemuel!"

Jesus smiled. "Lemuel, thank you for having us. You have a beautiful home." Jesus embraced him and kissed him on each cheek.

"Jesus of Nazareth! I have heard much about you. It is a blessing to have you, your friends, and your mother in my home.

I have rooms for all of you. Please come rest from your journey, and have something to eat and drink."

"That would be nice, but we have business at the temple." Jesus motioned toward Nathaniel and his disciples.

Lemuel said, "Of course. What was I thinking? Please let me know if you need anything while you're here. Enosh here is a good man. I will send him with you. Enosh, get them whatever they need," Lemuel told his servant.

"Yes, master." The servant bowed with respect.

"I will stay with your mother, and we will be here when you return," Gavriel said as he walked them back to the gate and the crowded streets of Jerusalem.

The temple wasn't far from Gavriel's home, and when they arrived, they walked into a chaotic storm of people. The court of the Gentiles made up the outer portion of the temple complex, where anyone could come, regardless of race or religion. Vendors were set up to change different currencies, and they charged a fee to do so. The Roman currency featured images of their gods, and the temple did not accept it, so money changers exchanged almost any currency for the silver half-shekel coin that the temple accepted. In addition to the money changers, sheep, goat, dove, and pigeon vendors were set up. Even though each family was to sacrifice an unblemished lamb, Levitical law allowed the poorer families to bring doves or even pigeons as a sacrifice if they couldn't find a group to join with a lamb.

Jesus stopped in the middle of the large court and watched the people and the vendors shouting at one another, all trying to get the best deal possible. "Jesus ... are you all right?" Nathaniel asked, watching his friend, who looked angry. Nathaniel thought for a moment and couldn't recall Jesus ever being angry.

"I'll be all right. Let's sit over there." Jesus pointed to a shaded spot next to the wall.

They all sat down, and Jesus began to fashion a whip out of some pieces of leather he had found in a pile of trash. No one said a word. They just watched Jesus and waited for him to start teaching. However, that never happened. He fixated on a poor couple trying to purchase a pigeon from a vendor. "Please, we only have these vegetables. We don't have any money. We just need one pigeon. Please help us. It's all we have."

"We don't barter. We just take money. Now get out of here!" The bird vendor picked up the vegetables and threw them at the couple. "Stinking Jews," he said under his breath but loud enough for those close by to hear. The couple crawled quickly to recover the food that the vendor threw at them. It was clearly all they had. The husband hung his head in shame as he comforted his wife.

"Teacher, please let me help." Enosh spoke to Jesus as he began to walk toward the couple. He purchased a dove for them from another vendor and blessed them and sent them on their way.

Just as Enosh turned around and started walking back toward the group, Jesus stood up and began to yell. "This is a house of prayer! You have turned it into a den of thieves! Do you not know the scripture?" He ran over to the bird vendor and swung the whip back and forth, turning over his table, being careful not to harm the birds. "Get out! Take your wares, and get out. This is a house of prayer!"

Nathaniel and the disciples just stood and watched, not believing what they saw. Jesus ran up and down the rows of vendors, yelling at them all and turning their tables over. Coins flew everywhere, and the men yelled back at him. "What's wrong with you? You're a crazy man! Who gives you the right?"

People shouted and tried to keep up with their lambs. Money changers scrambled, crawling on the ground, trying to keep track of their profits. Nathaniel ran up to Jesus and spun him around. "What are you doing? You can't do this!"

"Nathaniel, they are defiling my Father's house!"

"Your father? Jesus. What are you talking about? You've seen this same thing for years, and now, all of a sudden, you go crazy? Are you now trying to get us thrown out of Jerusalem?"

Nathaniel pleaded with him, and the crowd began to grow louder as the temple guard and some of the Jewish leaders approached.

"Who are you to do such a thing?" one of the leaders yelled at Jesus.

"Are you a divine prophet sent from God?" they mocked.

The crowd grew quiet so they could hear this exchange. Two men, Joseph of Arimathea and Nicodemus, both Pharisees, approached from the side and watched intently.

The other Jewish leaders continued. "Show us a sign. Come on; show us your authority!" they yelled.

Jesus just stood there. "This temple is a house of prayer, and this temple will be torn down and rebuilt in three days. That will be your sign."

"Three days ... three days? It took forty-six years to build this temple, and you are going to tear it down and rebuild it in three days!" They all began to laugh and make fun of Jesus. "He's a lunatic ... a madman! He's mad; come on." They waved him off, laughing at him and dismissing anything he said.

Joseph and Nicodemus just stood and watched Jesus, trying to figure out what he meant. But they knew he wasn't mad.

The disciples tried to calm Nathaniel down. "Nathaniel, it's okay. Let him go," Peter said.

"He's going to get us killed one day ... I just don't understand!" Nathaniel walked off angry, and the disciples walked over to Jesus. A crowd of people gathered around him, and he began to teach. The people disliked the vendors because they worked together with the high priests and leaders to cheat them and take their money. Anyone who stood up to them was a curiosity at best.

Peter and the other disciples sat at Jesus's side while he spoke. They had understood his anger at the vendors, and Andrew brought up that Jesus's attitude was written about by King David in the Psalms: "'Zeal for your house will consume me, and their insults will fall on me.'"

Nathaniel walked aimlessly through the crowd as the sun

95

began to set. He missed Sera. He missed Nazareth and his family, and he didn't understand why Jesus was such an amazing teacher but seemed to stir up trouble everywhere he went.

After a while, Jesus told the crowd he had to go but he would come back. He and the disciples looked for Nathaniel, but having no success, they headed back to Lemuel's home. Jesus took the disciples up onto the roof, gathered them around the fire, and began to teach them.

"Forgive me, Rabbi," Lemuel interrupted from the top of the stairs. "You have a guest."

Peter and the other disciples stood up quickly when Nicodemus, one of the Pharisees, climbed the last stairs onto the roof. They thought this might mean some repercussions from the events at the temple earlier. Jesus held up his hand to them, knowing why he had come.

"Rabbi, might I have a word with you?" Nicodemus called him Rabbi as a sign of respect, and it surprised Peter to hear a Pharisee call him by that name.

Peter looked back at Jesus, who told him, "It's okay, Peter. Thank you." Peter motioned for the other disciples to follow, and they all went downstairs with Lemuel.

"Please, Nicodemus, come sit with me." Jesus patted the cushion beside him.

Nicodemus was older and groaned a little. Jesus smiled and stretched out his hand to help him down. "Ah, thank you. These bones aren't getting any younger."

"What a pleasant surprise," Jesus said. "Peter and the others thought you might be here to reprimand me for what I did at the temple earlier." He spoke as he poured Nicodemus a cup of wine.

"Actually, the only thing I have to say about that is *bravo*! The vendors have gotten out of control, and it has become a pit of dishonesty. What you did needed to be done. Unfortunately, we all lacked the courage that you displayed today."

Nicodemus raised his cup to Jesus. "To your good health."

Jesus responded in kind and thanked him. Nicodemus stared at the fire when he spoke. "You know, I was there that day in the court of the Gentiles when you were young."

"Yes, I remember. You and Joseph of Arimathea were together. I couldn't forget."

Jesus listened to Nicodemus relive the moment. "I can never forget that day—a twelve-year-old boy from Nazareth putting the high priest and his successor in their place. It was a glorious day, indeed. Joseph and I knew that day that you were sent from God."

He hoped Jesus would respond to his revelation, but he didn't. Instead, he asked, "Nicodemus, why is it that you come to me at night?"

"Jesus, why do you ask questions that you already know the answer to?" They both laughed. "I know you're sent from God. No one can do the miracles you do without him." Nicodemus got right to the point. "You know I've been a teacher of the law for many years. I have studied my whole life and tried to live a life pleasing to God. From time to time, I receive new understanding on something I've read hundreds of times, and when that happens, it's a glorious moment!" Nicodemus's face lit up with excitement when he spoke. "It's almost like I'm speaking with God face-to-face, like Moses! Does that sound crazy?"

Jesus smiled. "No, my friend, it doesn't. God is pleased with you, Nicodemus—very pleased."

"You see, this is what I don't understand. When you speak, when you say things like that, I feel the same way, like God is ..." Nicodemus felt uncomfortable and looked around as if someone might be listening.

"Nicodemus, the truth is that unless you're born again, you won't see the kingdom of God."

"Born again?" Nicodemus queried. "Rabbi, how can an old man be born again? I cannot enter the womb a second time."

Jesus explained, "The truth is no one can enter the kingdom of heaven unless he is born of both water and the spirit. The flesh births flesh, and the spirit births spirit. Does this surprise you? Do you question the wind? It blows where it wishes, makes a sound, and you still don't know where it comes from or where it's going. It's the same with those born of the spirit!"

"How can this be? Rabbi, I don't understand."

"Nicodemus, you are a teacher of Israel. How is it you don't understand this simple truth? God loves this world so much he sent his only Son so that everyone would live and not die. All you have to do is believe! He came not to accuse you but so that you might have eternal life." They sat and talked, and Jesus continued to teach the great teacher.

"Rabbi, you have given me more than I can chew." Nicodemus chuckled as he strained to get up.

"Please let me help you." Jesus got up quickly and helped him up.

"Thank you." Nicodemus took Jesus's hands in his own. "Thank you for spending this time with me. I have much to think about." Nicodemus kissed Jesus on the head and looked him in the eyes. "Be careful; be careful with Caiaphas. He hasn't forgotten you, and he has not forgotten that day many years ago."

Nicodemus patted Jesus's hand like a grandfather might and turned to go down the stairs. He went down a few steps and turned back, steadying himself on the stairway wall. Jesus stood behind him at the top of the stairs, and the firelight reflected the somber look Jesus now had. "There are thousands upon thousands of people in Jerusalem, and out of all the Jews in this city, Caiaphas knows who you are. And that, my friend, is not a good thing. You watch yourself, Jesus of Nazareth. You watch yourself."

Nicodemus waved as he got to the bottom of the stairs, and Jesus walked across the roof toward the street, leaning against the railing. He watched Nicodemus walk away and waved when he looked back.

Jesus stayed at the rail just long enough to see Nathaniel coming through the gate a short time later. Nathaniel looked up and saw Jesus motion for him to come up. Nathaniel sat down near the fire, and neither of them spoke for a while.

"When I saw you go at it with Caiaphas and Annas in the temple that day, I knew our friendship would be special." Nathaniel paused, and Jesus didn't say anything. "I've never seen a man who loves God more than you do. You have a different understanding of who he is." Nathaniel waved his hand toward the sky and looked at the stars for a moment. Then he looked back at Jesus. "I don't understand the things you're doing. The temple, the miracles—how do you do those things? Why did God pick you—a guy from Nazareth? Why didn't he pick me? I love him."

Nathaniel broke up a small stick and threw the pieces forcefully into the fire. He was frustrated, and Jesus knew it. "You see, here's the thing; we've always been honest with each other, and to be honest with you, I'm scared. I'm scared that you are challenging the Jewish authorities. I'm scared that for the first time ever, I don't think you're being honest with me." Nathaniel looked across the fire and got no response. "It's not like I think you have lied to me or anything like that. I just think there's more to what's going on and you're not filling in the details."

Jesus leaned forward. "You're a wise man, my friend. There is more going on, and you will understand in time. God's timing is different than man's. You will have to trust me. I know you don't understand, but you will."

Jesus stirred the fire with a rod as he stood up. He walked over and lay down on a small pile of hay near the rail by the edge of the roof. Nathaniel sat for a while and thought about their conversation. He didn't have any more answers than before, but he would just have to stay the course and be strong. Eventually, his thoughts turned to his wife. He missed Sera and fell asleep thinking about when they would be together again.

CHAPTER 10

The night sky was beginning to fade to morning when Peter opened his eyes and saw Jesus kneeling over him. "Come on, Peter; wake the others. We have a lot to do today," Jesus said.

Peter tied on his sandals and said, "James, John, let's go. Get Nathaniel, Andrew, come on."

Jesus was already in the street outside the gate when a distant rooster began to crow. He paused and gathered the donkey carrying food. He was securing the last of the waterskins when Nathaniel came through the gate with the others.

Peter finished tying the water in place, saying, "Please, let me, Rabbi."

Jesus looked up, smiled, and ruffled Andrew's hair a bit. "Wake up, my friend." Andrew half smiled, peering through the morning sun and rubbing sleep from his eyes. "We have to go to Capernaum. A man is waiting for us there," Jesus said, leading the donkey toward the hill country.

James spoke up and motioned to John to look behind them. "Jesus, several people are following us." Several men and a few women with children followed at a distance behind them down the dusty road.

"Yes, I know; they are coming with us. Come on!" Jesus laughed and waved for them to catch up. The group behind all ran up to them, excited to be accepted as part of the group.

"Good morning, Rabbi," one man said. He was out of breath from running to catch up.

"Good morning, brother." Jesus greeted them all with a smile and embraced them one by one.

"We are going to Capernaum, if you would like to join us." Peter joined in and welcomed the group.

"Yes, that would be great. Thank you," another man responded.

Once they reached the edge of the city, Jesus began to teach. They walked for miles, and Jesus taught them on loving others and the importance of loving your neighbor as God loves us.

The sun high in the sky, they stopped and sat in the shade of a stone outcropping for lunch. Jesus sat on a rock, and everyone sat on the ground around him. They all talked and introduced themselves to each other.

"Pangi," one of the women called out, but it was too late. The little girl escaped her mother's grasp, ran, and stood behind Jesus. "Teacher, I'm sorry. Pangi, leave the teacher alone."

"Please, it's okay." Jesus laughed and waved his hand, welcoming the child. "Hello, Pangi," Jesus said, looking back toward her. She was about five years old and had dark skin and bright hazel eyes.

"Hello," she said while she reached over and began to straighten and arrange Jesus's hair.

"Pangi! Teacher, I'm so sorry," the mother said. Her face turned red, and she fidgeted with embarrassment.

Jesus smiled at her and repeated, "It's okay." The little girl pulled his hair up to her nose and smelled it with a strange look on her face. Then she put her whole face into his hair, took a deep breath, and stepped back with a big grin. She walked around beside him, put one hand on her hip, and waved her other finger at Jesus.

"Did you put honey in your hair? Your hair smells just like honey!" she exclaimed. She walked back around him and continued to play with and smell his hair. Everyone burst out laughing.

Pangi's mom covered her face. "Oh, Pangi … Pangi."

Jesus laughed and reached around behind him and took her by the hand. "Pangi, come have something to eat with me," Jesus said.

"Okay," she said, fluffing his hair. She gently gathered two tiny handfuls of his hair, smelling it one last time.

From his bag, he laid out dried fish, crusty bread, and figs on a cloth in front of them. Pangi sat close to him on the rock. Jesus took out his waterskin and took a big drink. He looked down at Pangi swallowing his water. "Hm?" He motioned to her as he took another drink. She nodded in affirmation, and Jesus helped her by holding the skin as she drank.

Everyone ate, and Pangi laid her head on Jesus's lap and fell into a deep sleep. He leaned his back up against the tree, closed his eyes, and prayed for this child and her future as a woman of God, full of love.

After a short rest, he cradled the sleeping child in his arms, brushed the hair out of her face, picked her up, and laid her up on the donkey between the supplies and blankets. "Come. We need to go." He spoke quietly so as not to wake the little girl.

They traveled until dark and then built a fire and set up a watch for the night. With robbers and thieves on the road, it was wise to keep a lookout just in case.

Jesus lay down by Nathaniel. "I thought we could go through Nazareth tomorrow. I'm sure things have settled down by now. What do you think?" Jesus asked his friend.

"That's a good plan. I miss her."

"I know you do, Nathaniel. Get some rest."

★★★

They got an early start the next day and split up when they got to the road to Nazareth. "Peter, you go ahead, and I will meet you at Gavriel's house in two days." Jesus embraced his disciples and encouraged the group to go with Peter. Jesus and Nathaniel waved as the group headed for Capernaum with the donkey and supplies. They were just a few hours from Nazareth, and they kept one waterskin between them.

"Okay, how about a different plan this time?" Nathaniel slapped Jesus on the back lightly.

"What do you mean?" Jesus asked, knowing full well what he was suggesting.

"Might I suggest we try something other than the 'provoking everyone to a rage and getting us thrown out of town' approach?"

Jesus just rolled his eyes and shook his head. "Come on."

They came into Nazareth close to Nathaniel's parents' home and couldn't get through the gate before Sera came running and embraced her husband with tears in her eyes.

Yona and Seth came out, and everyone greeted each other with hugs and kisses on the cheek. Jesus was noticeably quiet. Seth turned to Jesus to embrace him. "I'm not sure what all of that was about in the synagogue, but you're as much a son to us as Nathaniel. Let's move on and forget about it."

"Thank you. I love you both." Jesus reached out and hugged them again. "You two have perfect timing. I just got a large furniture order from Capernaum and could use two young carpenters to finish up." Jesus laughed, and Nathaniel smiled and rolled his eyes. He kissed Sera, and they headed to the shop. The three men worked the rest of the day, and together, they finished the furniture order.

"You know, I'm headed to Capernaum in a couple of days. I'm happy to deliver your order," Jesus said, wiping the sweat from his arms and face.

Seth agreed. "That would be great!"

"Sera and I can go also. It will be nice to take her and spend time together. Hey, are these cushions new?" Nathaniel was about to sit back on a chair when the door to the shop opened.

Sera appeared just in time. "Don't you dare! I have fresh water in a bowl outside for you to wash up before you touch those cushions."

Jesus caught Nathaniel's hand and pulled him up just before he sat down completely. Jesus advised his friend, "Come on; you're about to get into some trouble."

Nathaniel sighed. "All right, all right."

Sera swatted at Nathaniel with a towel as he walked by, and Jesus raised his eyebrows and jokingly walked sideways through the door to avoid her. They quickly cleaned up, sat in the shop, and caught up on the day. They pulled back the window coverings and felt the refreshing breeze.

"Sera, why don't you go to Capernaum with us? We can take the furniture for Father, and Jesus has some things to do there also." Nathaniel looked at her, hoping she would agree.

"Of course, I'm going. Someone has to keep you two out of trouble. And yes, Nathaniel already told me about the money changers at the temple." Sera crossed her arms and looked at Jesus.

"Oh, about that ..." Nathaniel shrugged his shoulders.

"Thanks a lot, Nathaniel!" Jesus chided.

After that, they joined Seth and Yona for dinner on the roof. Nathaniel told them about their adventures. For the time being, everything was back to normal.

The next morning, they woke up early, loaded the furniture onto a cart, and hitched it behind an ox. "Be back in a couple of days," Nathaniel called out as they headed back down the road to Capernaum. Jesus led the ox while Sera and Nathaniel sat on the back of the cart and talked most of the way.

As they entered the town, word spread fast, and crowds began to gather around them. "See, I told you. He's famous all through the hill country." Nathaniel could see the look of disbelief on Sera's face.

"Come on, you two. We've been invited to dinner!" Jesus had his arm around a man, walking toward a home by the water.

Nathaniel tied up the ox, and he and Sera joined Jesus inside the house. Lots of people were in the home, and food and wine were passed around.

Nathaniel and Sera sat in the corner and watched as Jesus began to teach. When Peter and the disciples arrived, the room became extremely crowded. People came in through the windows, and it was standing room only. Although the crowd was enormous, it stayed very quiet as everyone watched to see if Jesus would do a miracle.

Suddenly, there came a banging on the ceiling, and dried mud and straw began to fall on people near Jesus. A clearing formed where the clay fell, and men started frantically digging, making a large hole in the roof.

One of the servants yelled out, "Hey, what are you doing?"

"Leave them!" Jesus instructed.

After the hole grew large enough, a man tied to his bed was lowered down through the hole. His bed rested on the roof debris. The man just lay there, looking at Jesus. Some Sadducees and Pharisees sat nearby and watched carefully to see what Jesus would do next. Jesus looked over at them, turned back toward the paralyzed man, and said, "Your sins are forgiven."

Nathaniel cringed. "Relax," Sera said as she reached over and grabbed his hand.

Nathaniel quietly asked her, "What is he doing? Why is he talking like that?" He felt nervous because he knew this was how things started out in the synagogue in Nazareth.

Sera reassured him, "Let's just wait and see."

The Pharisees and teachers of the law began to grumble among themselves. Jesus looked at them and turned toward Nathaniel. "Why are you questioning in your hearts what I just said?" Jesus looked at Nathaniel for a moment and then turned back toward the Sadducees and Pharisees. "Which is easier to say: your sins are forgiven, or stand up and walk?"

Jesus looked back at Nathaniel and then around the room. "So you will realize that the son of man has the power to forgive sins on earth, I tell you rise and walk!" Jesus addressed the paralyzed man.

The man had a look of surprise and confusion on his face and began to move beneath the blanket that covered him. Those who knew him gasped and began to praise God.

Jesus said to those near him, "Untie him."

They untied the man, and he stood up, slowly testing his legs with a smile, tears welling up in his eyes. He looked up at his friends through the hole in the roof, raised his hands, and said, "Look, I can walk! I can walk!"

Sera said, "Nathaniel, Jesus healed him! He healed him!" The room filled with fear and joy. No one in the room had ever seen anything like this before. "Nathaniel! Nathaniel! Did you see that? He healed him." Sera kept repeating the same thing over and over.

Jesus looked at the teachers of the law, who had a mixed reaction of rage and awe. Several of them got up and pushed their way out of the room. The man took up his bed and was about to follow them when he turned back to Jesus. He walked over to Jesus, took his hand, and kissed it. "Thank you. I have no other words but thank you," he said quietly with tears streaming down his face.

His friends yelled now from the doorway, "Come on!" The man looked back at them and smiled and then looked back at Jesus, not wanting to leave.

"Go." Jesus smiled and motioned toward his friends.

"Thank you! Thank you!" The man began to laugh, picked up his bed, and walked quickly toward his friends. The crowd parted to watch him walk, and they congratulated him, embracing him as he went through the crowd.

Jesus stood up and looked for Nathaniel and Sera. They were trying to reach him, but the crowd pressed in around him and made it hard to move. Finally, things began to lighten up, and Jesus convinced the crowd he wasn't leaving Capernaum and they had to find a bigger place for him to continue teaching.

The disciples followed Jesus out of the house, and they all headed toward the market. The crowd followed Jesus as he walked through the streets, and they could here people talking about him and the miracle he had just performed.

The crowd of people crushed in on Jesus as he walked toward the tax office. There, a man stood in the doorway. He looked at Jesus. The teacher walked up to the man and simply said, "Follow me," and the man did. Peter looked at James and John, and they all shrugged their shoulders. This seemed commonplace after the miracle they had just witnessed.

"Peter, this is Matthew," Jesus said, introducing them.

The two new friends embraced, and Matthew whispered to Peter, "How does he know my name?"

Peter laughed and whispered back, "Come on. You haven't seen anything yet." Matthew was bewildered, but he knew he should go with them.

Jesus looked back and then slowed down to walk beside Nathaniel and Sera. He walked between them, arm in arm.

"Jesus, how did you do that?" Sera asked in amazement.

Jesus smiled. "I just do the will of my Father, and he honors my obedience and my faith."

She asked with a look of confusion, "You mean … Joseph?"

"No, silly, Joseph is dead. My Father in heaven!" Jesus laughed and ran to climb a hill they had come to outside of town. Jesus yelled back to them, climbing steadily toward the top, "Come on; it's lunchtime!"

They had walked outside of town, and the crowd of people had grown even larger. People from all over joined them. They wanted to see something miraculous or to be healed. Some thought Jesus was a powerful prophet sent from God, and rumors spread that he might even be the Messiah.

Jesus sat down, looked around at the enormous crowd, and had compassion for them. Some of them had traveled with him for several days, and he knew their food and supplies were running out. Jesus looked over the crowd and said, "Peter, we need to feed these people."

"Rabbi, how could we possibly feed a crowd like this? I think we have a few small fish and six or seven loaves of bread."

"Bring all of it to me," Jesus said.

The disciples were excited and quickly brought the fish and bread. Nathaniel, Sera, and the disciples stood and watched as Jesus prayed and broke the bread and fish into pieces. They watched even more intently after he prayed, but nothing happened. The group looked up at Jesus and back down again. Nothing happened.

Jesus said insistently, "Well, go ... go feed them!" They divided the seven baskets among themselves and looked at each other hesitantly. Each basket either had a few pieces of bread or several small pieces of bread in it. Jesus motioned toward the crowd. "Come on; have faith. Go!"

"Okay, here we go." Nathaniel left first and walked toward the group of people sitting nearest to him, and the others did the same, walking in different directions. Nathaniel was almost to the group when he felt a weight in the basket and tumbled forward. He didn't have enough time to catch himself and fell face-first into the basket and toward the rock. He cringed and tightened up, preparing for the impact, and was pleasantly surprised when he stopped short. The full basket of warm, fresh bread, which he now lay facedown in, cushioned his fall. He rolled over, and everyone laughed, seeing he was all right. He stared down at the big pile of bread in his lap and all around him. Nathaniel laughed with them and said, "Well, come on; help yourselves."

Everyone jumped up eagerly, grabbed the bread, and began to pass it around. Nathaniel watched as two men took his basket and began to run through the crowd, throwing bread out to everyone. He looked over at Sera and watched her laugh in amazement as she handed out bread in an unending supply. Nathaniel loved to watch her laugh and couldn't remember a happier moment in his life. The two of them made eye contact, and Sera tried to hold up her basket with another woman. They both laughed and praised God. Nathaniel smiled and waved two loaves at her, one in each hand.

Nathaniel turned and looked at Jesus, who stood a short distance away. He was smiling when he turned toward Nathaniel. Nathaniel smiled back and began to laugh when Matthew and Peter dropped several whole fish in his lap from a basket they both struggled to carry. Matthew almost fell trying to help carry the basket to the next group. "Can you believe it?"

"Yes … yes, I can believe it," Nathaniel said quietly, surveying the crowd while they praised God and gave thanks. He looked back at Jesus and raised his loaf toward him. Jesus looked back, smiled, and did the same.

After a while, Jesus sent the crowds away, and most of them left except for a group of about a hundred who said they wanted to become his disciples.

Sera and some ladies gathered up the rest of the leftover food, and Nathaniel joined Jesus and the group of disciples. He had missed much of what Jesus taught them, and when he got there, some of the Jews were upset and talking among themselves. Nathaniel just heard a little bit of the conversation from a distance, about a miracle and wanting bread from heaven.

"You say you want bread from heaven, and I tell you I am that bread sent from God." The crowd groaned when Jesus said this. "I tell you now to receive this gift that my Father has sent you. He has sent you his Son from above to be the bread of eternal life. I am that bread. Unless you eat my body and drink my blood, I cannot raise you up on the last day into eternal life." Jesus spoke figuratively, but most of the crowd could not discern the spiritual meaning of this saying. They discussed it for a short time, and one by one, most of them left. Nathaniel just stood there, angry and confused. He dropped the last piece of bread in his hand and walked away with the crowd, looking for Sera.

"Nathaniel!" Jesus called out. "Nathaniel, wait. Let me …"

Nathaniel swung around quickly. "Let you what? Let you what?" Nathaniel yelled. "I can't take this anymore; it's craziness! You just now said you're the Son of God. Jesus ... the Son of God. You just told a group of men they had to eat your flesh and drink your blood! They came to you for spiritual guidance, and the best you have to offer is for them to drink your blood?"

Sera came running up when she heard Nathaniel yelling. "Nathaniel, please calm down."

Peter tried to intervene. Nathaniel screamed, and Peter backed away. "Don't tell me to calm down. I won't calm down!" Nathaniel was red in the face and pacing back and forth, breathing heavily. "I thought you were my friend. I've always been there for you—always!" Tears began to stream down his face as he yelled, "You got me kicked out of my home, and I even had to leave my wife. You almost got us killed, and rumor has it Caiaphas hates you! The high priest, Jesus—the high priest hates you! Why you say some of the things you do, I will never know. Most of your disciples left, and your own brothers and sisters have turned against you. I don't know how you do some of the things you've done, but I know these people come to you to learn more about the law. Then you do and say these crazy things!" Nathaniel took several deep breaths and wiped his face with his tunic.

Jesus said, "Nathaniel, please—"

"No, I've made up my mind. I can't do this anymore. I'm taking a job near Jerusalem. I'm going to do some work for the Romans."

Sera spoke out. "Nathaniel?"

"Not right now, Sera!" he said sternly.

Matthew said, "Nathaniel, please!"

"Stop! All of you, stop!" Nathaniel shouted. "Just leave me alone. I've had enough." He lowered his voice, turned, and awkwardly said to Jesus, "I'll see you ... sometime." He walked away, taking Sera by the arm, and headed for the group farther down the road.

Peter begged, "Lord, please let me go after him!"

"No, Peter. Let him go—just let him go," Jesus said softly, tears welling up in his eyes. "Let's gather our things. Lazarus is sick and needs my help."

CHAPTER 11

Months earlier, Jesus had met Mary, Martha, and Lazarus, three siblings, while visiting Jerusalem. They welcomed him into their home. He and the disciples stayed there sometimes when they were in the area. The three siblings loved Jesus and traveled with him frequently. One time, however, they stayed back because Lazarus didn't feel well.

When Martha heard Jesus was coming back, she ran to meet him when he was still a short distance from Bethany, the small village just outside of Jerusalem where they lived. With tears in her eyes, she pleaded, "Lord, if you had only been here …"

"Yes, Martha, I know what has happened," Jesus responded, embracing her and trying to comfort her a little. "It's all right. Lazarus will rise again."

She replied, "I know he will rise in the resurrection, but—"

Jesus stopped and looked at her. "I am the resurrection and the life. All you have to do is believe in me, and even though you might die, you will live. Can you believe this?"

Tearful, Martha answered, "Lord, I believe you are … the Christ sent from God. I believe whatever you ask will be done."

Several of the Jews standing nearby began to grumble. Martha felt as if Jesus was about to do something when she ran to get her sister. Mary almost lifelessly sat in a chair. Her eyes looked swollen from crying, and she was angry, knowing that Jesus could have saved Lazarus.

"Mary, come quick; he's here." Martha pulled Mary out of the chair, out the door, and through the gate. All the Jews sitting around her quickly followed until they all came to the place where Jesus had met Martha near the tomb.

Mary wept when she fell at Jesus's feet. "Lord, Lord, if only you had been here!"

Jesus looked around at the Jews and then back at Mary and Martha. He groaned inside his spirit because they still didn't understand. Jesus walked toward the tomb and told the men to remove the stone.

Martha said quietly to Jesus, "Lord, he's been there four days. There will be a bad smell by now."

Jesus gently took her by the shoulders and said, "Martha, you must believe what I'm telling you. If you believe, you will see the glory of God."

The men grumbled as they rolled away the stone and stepped back from the tomb. No one said a word. Once again, all eyes were on Jesus. He looked around at the crowd and sensed their apprehension and, in some, unbelief. He groaned inside, knowing how things should really be, there and then. If Adam had just listened in the garden, perfection and love would surround them, and Lazarus would not be dead.

Jesus looked up toward heaven. "Father, I thank you that you have heard my prayer. I thank you that you would do this so those who are here will believe that you sent me." Jesus shouted, "Lazarus!" and startled the bystanders. Everyone watched the darkness of the open tomb. "Lazarus!" He shouted again, "Come out!"

A stirring came from inside the tomb, and then, a figure emerged from the darkness and stood at the opening. The hot Judean sun illuminated the white burial wrappings. Several people screamed, and some ran away. Many of the Jews bowed down on the ground in fear and awe. Martha and Mary froze in place and couldn't move. Time seemed to stop. They were both startled when Jesus spoke again. "Go, free your brother." He looked around at the crowd. "Go, free him!"

The women began to laugh as they ran to help him. Several of the skeptics just sat back and watched the whole thing transpire, and Jesus watched them leave quickly and hurry back toward Jerusalem.

The witnesses arrived at the temple and pushed their way through the crowds. When they reached the council, in the shade of the porch, the temple guard stopped them.

"Let them through," Annas commanded the soldiers.

Caiaphas spoke rudely to the men, who were sweaty and out of breath. "I assume you have news for us! Make it quick; we are in session." Caiaphas had been appointed high priest, to follow Annas, his father-in-law. However, Caiaphas was just a puppet. Annas had the real control and made most of the decisions.

One of the men spoke up. "High Priest, something has happened—something we can't explain."

"Well, what is it? Hurry up!" Caiaphas yelled.

"It's Jesus. Jesus of Nazareth."

"Great, what now! Can I not escape the name Jesus of Nazareth?" Caiaphas sat down and began to eat some dates. "Go on! Go on!" He nodded to the guard, who, in turn, shoved the sweaty man to the ground with his spear.

The man winced in pain and quickly got to his feet. He said, "We were in Bethany last week and discovered Jesus's friend, Lazarus of Bethany, was sick. We heard his sisters send messengers to bring back Jesus from Capernaum. He could have easily returned to Bethany in a couple of days. But he didn't come until after Lazarus died. High Priest, I tell you we witnessed the next part with our own eyes, and every word is true."

Caiaphas looked at the guard as if to ask him why the man was still standing. The guard struck the man in the ribs with the flat of his sword and cut his arm in the process. Caiaphas yelled, "Get on with it, and don't bleed on my floor!"

"Yes, High Priest." The man tried to catch his breath while he pulled up his tunic to wrap his arm. Several Pharisees came in and sat down to listen.

"Lazarus died. We saw his family put him in the grave. They rolled a large stone in front of the tomb. The tomb appeared undisturbed for four days, and that's when Jesus arrived." The man was in obvious pain and hesitated for a moment, not wanting to tell the rest of the story. This sent Caiaphas into a rage. Caiaphas looked up, annoyed at the man's hesitation as he moved quickly away from the guard. "I'm sorry. Please …" He stumbled and fell to the ground, curling up into the fetal position to absorb the impending blow from the guard.

"Stop!" Annas spoke up. Caiaphas exhaled loudly with displeasure and spat out a date seed at the man. "If you would continue, please." Annas glared at Caiaphas, who pretended not to notice.

"Thank you, Rabbi." The man slowly stood up and continued with the story. "The stone … it hadn't been disturbed, and the man, Lazarus, had been in the grave four days. We saw them put him in there after he died. They were all mourning—men and women alike."

The man hesitated and suddenly cowered when Caiaphas yelled, "Would you please get on with it! I'm growing old listening to you babbling on!"

The poor man winced and shook his head, knowing what would happen if he finished the story, but he continued anyway, weighing what would certainly happen if he didn't. "Jesus told the men to roll the stone away from the tomb. Even Lazarus's sister cautioned him that the body would smell. When they rolled it away, Jesus looked up at the sky, said something, and then yelled for Lazarus to come out, and nothing happened. He yelled a second time, and the dead man walked out of the tomb. He was bound in burial clothes. Fifty people were there to witness what happened. I'm not making this up." The man backed away from the guards and from Caiaphas.

The high priest didn't have a chance to react when one of the council spoke up. "It's true! At least that's what the word is on the street. Forgive us; we came in late, but everyone in town is talking about this. Lazarus of Bethany is alive and well."

Caiaphas screamed and threw his bowl of dates at the man and his friends. "This is nonsense! Get them out of here!" This time, Annas sat back and let Caiaphas carry on. "There is no resurrection from the dead or rising from the dead, and if God decided to empower a prophet to resurrect the dead, he wouldn't use a carpenter from Nazareth!" Caiaphas screamed and threw his chair toward the temple guards standing nearby. "This Jesus ... he is deceiving the people of Jerusalem. He's going to start a rebellion. And when Rome gets involved, it will be the end of us. Do you hear me? The end of us!"

Both Sadducees and Pharisees seemed to agree. Once Caiaphas realized his fear tactic was working, he carefully laid out his plan. "Is this what you want, for one man to destroy Jerusalem and for the Roman authorities to dissolve this council and destroy everything we've worked so hard toward?" Caiaphas strutted around, manipulating the council and bringing them in agreement with his vengeful plan. "No, we won't let that happen!"

When he raised his voice, some of them responded, "No, we won't!"

He continued. "No, we are God's people. No one man will tear us down and deliver us to the judgment of the Romans! The people are more important than one man. If one man must die for the many, then so be it!"

Caiaphas had worked them into a frenzy, and they raised their voices in agreement. "Kill him! He must be sacrificed for the many!" Many of them could be heard chanting.

Annas just smiled and sat back, watching Caiaphas perform. He had taught Caiaphas well.

After a few minutes, the council got quiet. Joseph of Arimathea spoke up. "Caiaphas, do we judge Jewish men before they are heard?" Even Caiaphas respected Joseph, a Pharisee. He had enormous influence in the council and was not someone to dismiss lightly. "Jesus has not been heard, and to condemn a man without a trial goes against everything we teach."

Caiaphas decided to push the matter a bit. "Joseph, surely you haven't become a believer, have you?"

Joseph replied, "Condemning a man who has done wrong is one thing. However, if there is truth to anything he is doing, we will find ourselves fighting against God himself."

There was complete silence in the room, and Annas was about to speak up when Caiaphas said, "Joseph, you are a highly respected member of this council, and we appreciate your wisdom. Your suggestion has been taken under advisement. However, I have decided we will proceed, since the majority of this council seems to agree with me. Jesus of Nazareth will die!"

Joseph sat back beside his friend Nicodemus and shook his head. And from that time forward, the rest of them began plotting to have Jesus killed.

CHAPTER 12

Sera called out from the rooftop, "Nathaniel, your lunch is ready."

"I'll be right up," Nathaniel said, scraping off the bark of a large log.

He had been making beams for the Romans for a week. His contact, Atticus, was kind enough. Kindness was unusual for any Roman soldier dealing with a Jew. Atticus was actually more of a merchant than a soldier. Even Sera liked him.

Nathaniel had met a young man named Herut. Together, they had almost finished the Romans' order. Nathaniel said to his new apprentice, "Come on. Let's wash up. We can finish later."

Herut asked respectfully, "Master, what are the Romans building with these beams?"

"To be honest, Herut, I don't make a habit of questioning the Romans about anything. You should make that your practice as well."

"Agreed, master." They both laughed.

The building where they were staying was owned by the Romans. It had a makeshift courtyard where they would shape logs into beams and load them onto carts. The Romans had picked up one order several days before and were due to pick up another order the next day.

Sera had just come down with their lunch and set it on a

tree stump near where they were washing up by the street when someone called out from the street, "Hello, Nathaniel."

Nathaniel waved at his friend. "Sirus! I haven't seen you in a few days. Everything all right?"

"Yes, everything is good. I had to go to Jerusalem and pick up a few things. It took me twice as long to get through the city as usual. Some sort of commotion was going on with the Sanhedrin and Pontius Pilate. Some poor soul was getting executed," Sirus said.

Nathaniel responded casually while washing his hands. "Isn't that a weekly occurrence with the Romans?"

"That's true, but this man must have committed some horrible crime. They paraded him through the streets. They had put a ring of thorns on his head and beaten him so badly that you could barely recognize him as a man. It was terrible."

Nathaniel dried his face and tossed the towel to Herut. "Well, let's hope the punishment fit the crime."

"I suppose so. Why don't you come down after you eat? I brought back some dates."

Sera waved goodbye to Sirus and said, "We will, Sirus. Thank you."

Nathaniel tied a large tarp between three poles and made a canopy for them to sit under and eat. Sera set the tray of food down between the two of them and brought some cups and a jug of water. They sat and ate quietly. Sera had been quiet for several days. She really hadn't had much to say since they got to Bethlehem. Nathaniel knew she didn't approve of his working for the Romans, and she wanted him to go make peace with Jesus. They had been friends since they were children, and Sera had never seen them at odds.

Nathaniel broke the silence. "So, are we going to talk about this?"

Sera reached out for his hand. "He's your best friend. You've known him all your life."

"I know, but he's keeping things from me, and all this nonsense he's been talking about. He even said he was sent here to die for us. Does that sound crazy? It's not just me."

Herut squirmed and was ready to jump up. "Master, should I go?"

Nathaniel waved for him to sit. "No, you're fine." He leaned toward his wife. "Sera, Peter and the others are calling him the Messiah, the Christ!" Nathaniel threw his hands up and then sat back and looked at her. "What am I missing?"

She looked hard at him. "Nathaniel, what if you're wrong, and what if Peter and the others are right?"

"Sera! Do you know what you are saying? That I used to play games with the Messiah when I was young, that the men in Nazareth tried to kill the Christ, and that the high priest and the Sanhedrin hate the Messiah? Sera, please, not you too." Nathaniel stood up and paced back and forth. Herut jumped up and began to clear away the dishes, and Nathaniel let him.

Sera stood up close to him, took his hands, and looked up at him. "I don't know what's going on or why he is doing these things. You have to admit that God has done some amazing things through him, things like the old prophets used to do, things that have not happened in hundreds of years. I met a woman who just came from Bethany in the market. She said Lazarus died from his sickness and Jesus brought him back to life. She and her husband and his brothers saw the whole thing. Please, let's at least go talk with him, just the three of us. He will tell us. I know he will."

Nathaniel hugged his wife and stared out toward the desert behind the house. "All right, we'll go talk with him. We will leave after the order is picked up tomorrow."

Sera smiled and hugged him tight. "Thank you!" She kissed him on the cheek and ran back toward the stairs leading to the roof.

Nathaniel gathered a few tools and said, "Herut, come on. Let's get this finished."

It took them an hour to shape the final few beams and to load the last of them onto the cart. "Let's clean up and go down to Sirus's house, and when we get back, we need to pack our things. We are going to Jerusalem tomorrow," Nathaniel said.

"Master, if you don't mind, I can stay here and get everything packed. It will be ready when you get back."

Nathaniel agreed. "That's a good idea, Herut. Thank you."

Sera came back downstairs. She and Nathaniel walked the short distance up the street to their friends' house. Myrium, Sirus's wife, waved as they walked through the gate and across the shaded courtyard. Myrium greeted Nathaniel and kissed Sera on the cheek as they sat down at a table with wine and a large bowl of dates.

Sirus greeted his guests and walked toward the gate as two men walked in. "Hello, Rabbi. Rabbi, please meet my friends. This is Nathaniel and his wife, Sera."

The rabbi responded, "Shalom. Pleased to meet you all. This is my son, Mikhos."

Sirus insisted, "Please, everyone sit down. Make yourselves at home." Everyone sat down on cushions under a big tree growing in the middle of the courtyard. Sera and Myrium made sure everyone had wine, and they sat down.

"Ah! These dates are so sweet! Thank you!" The rabbi grabbed a few more from the large bowl sitting on the ground between them all.

Sirus laughed. "I thought you might like them. So, what did we miss at the synagogue this morning? I hated to miss our daily discussion, but I was traveling back from Jerusalem."

The rabbi patted his son on the shoulder. "Mikhos came from Jerusalem today also. I don't know how you missed each other." Reaching for more dates, the rabbi said, "We discussed the Messiah this morning." Sera looked at Nathaniel, and then Nathaniel smiled and shook his head in disbelief. The rabbi queried, "What did I say?"

"Well, we were just talking about that very same topic before we came over here today," Nathaniel answered while Sera poured him some more wine.

"We studied the prophet Isaiah this morning. I believe a certain portion speaks about the Messiah."

"What portion, Rabbi?" Nathaniel asked.

"I will quote it: 'My servant grew up in the Lord's presence like a tender green shoot, like a root in dry ground. There was nothing beautiful or majestic about his appearance, nothing to attract us to him. He was despised and rejected—a man of sorrows, acquainted with deepest grief. We turned our backs on him and looked the other way. He was despised, and we did not care. Yet it was our weaknesses he carried; it was our sorrows that weighed him down. And we thought his troubles were a punishment from God, a punishment for his own sins!'"

No one saw Sera whisper to Nathaniel, "This is not a coincidence! We need to find him."

Mikhos spoke up. "You know that teacher in Jerusalem was arrested because he said he was the Messiah."

Nathaniel froze. "What teacher?" He could barely get the words out.

"The Nazarene. Where have you been? The whole world is talking about him." Mikhos reached for a few dates. "It was tragic, really. His name was Jesus ... Jesus of Nazareth."

Nathaniel's stomach sank, and he dropped his cup, spilling wine all over his tunic.

"No!" Sera exclaimed quietly. Both her hands covered her mouth as tears began to form in her eyes.

The rabbi asked, "What? Do you know this man?"

"Yes, we know him. I'm sorry; we have to leave." Nathaniel jumped up quickly and pulled Sera to her feet, and they both ran toward the gate.

"Nathaniel, Sera ... what's wrong? Nathaniel!" Sirus chased after them to the street, but neither of them responded as they continued to run down the street.

"Herut! Herut! We have to leave now!" Nathaniel yelled as they came through the gate.

"Yes, master." Herut ran and got the donkey and loaded her with water.

"Maybe it's not him," Sera said as she rushed around putting food in a basket. "Jesus is a common name." Sera was frightened and chattered nervously while packing necessities for the trip.

Herut watched his master uneasily. Nathaniel knew this would be a frustrating trip, feeling the panic he felt inside. He grabbed the donkey's reins and began to walk quickly toward the gate. Suddenly, the stubborn animal stopped and started pulling him backward. Nathaniel caught his balance and turned quickly toward the donkey. He raised his hand in anger and then paused. He closed his eyes for a moment, took a deep breath, reached out, and rubbed the animal's head. "Sorry, old girl. Let's go." This time, they proceeded at her pace.

Donkeys never get going in a hurry, and to get angry and scold these animals is pointless. Herut and Sera let out a sigh of relief when Nathaniel softly placed his hand on the donkey's head. He was never cruel to animals, but they had never seen him this worried before.

They set out for Jerusalem and traveled all night, saying few words. The sun rose as they went through the city gate. Jerusalem was beginning to stir, and people began to fill the streets.

Nathaniel, Sera, and Herut made their way to Gavriel's house. When they arrived, Nathaniel ran through the gate. Peter and the others saw him coming and ran out to meet him.

"Where is he?" Nathaniel was wide-eyed and scared, looking around for his friend.

Peter tried to calm him. "Nathaniel, they took him—"

"I know they took him! Where is he?" he screamed back in a rage, tears forming in his eyes.

"Nathaniel?" Matthew and the others suddenly realized Nathaniel had no idea what happened.

"Golgotha … After the trial, they took him to Golgotha." John spoke quietly with the intention of comforting him.

"No! No!" Nathaniel screamed and ran toward the gate. He didn't open the gate all the way, and his tunic got caught on the fence, partially tearing it and sending him crashing down onto the dusty street. He hit his head, and blood began to mix with the dirt on the right side of his face.

Nathaniel ran through the street like a madman. "Get out of the way!" he yelled, pushing his way through the crowd. He ran into the back of a couple and knocked the woman to the ground. Before Nathaniel could say a word, her husband grabbed him and threw him across the narrow street into a fruit cart, knocking the breath out of him and cutting his leg. By this time, several others he pushed had caught up, and they all began to kick and punch him. They all assumed he was just some lunatic running through the streets.

Sera and the disciples caught up to him and yelled at the crowd, moving in to protect him. During the chaos, Nathaniel got up and limped through the mayhem toward the hill. He almost reached the top when Peter and the rest caught up to him. Peter reached out and grabbed the bottom of Nathaniel's robe. It was covered with dirt and blood and tore again even worse than before. Nathaniel limped and winced in pain as he breathed. One of the men in the streets landed a crushing blow to his abdomen and probably broke at least one of his ribs.

"Nathaniel, stop. Stop. We have to tell you …" When Sera and the men got to the top of the hill, they stood behind him. Nathaniel stared at a cross that lay on the ground. It had a sign nailed to the top of it: "Jesus of Nazareth, King of the Jews."

Nathaniel fell to his knees and began crying. Sera ran to him and cried beside him on the ground. He fell forward, hugged the base of the cross, and ran his hands over the wood. "No, no, no …!" Nathaniel stopped rubbing the wood and sat up with his eyes locked on the wooden beam he had lain on. All the color drained from his face, and he fought wave after wave of nausea. He tried to speak to the disciples, and even Sera couldn't figure out what had changed.

"Nathaniel?" Sera tried to reach out for him, but he backed away quickly, kicking the dirt and rocks.

"No. Oh my God, no!" Nathaniel could barely get the words out. He tried to get up but fell back down in pain, only taking his eyes off the cross for a moment.

Peter and Andrew carefully helped him to his feet. "Nathaniel, what—?"

"Help me," he interrupted, limping to the crossbeam. He reached down and saw the nail covered with his friend's blood. He needed to turn the cross over, but his head was spinning, and he fell to one knee and just stared at the bloody hole the nail made when it was hammered through Jesus's hand into the wood.

His last conversation with the Romans kept playing over and over in his head. "What am I making?" he asked the legion officer.

"Does it really matter? We need beams of wood in these two lengths, and you need a job. You make the beams, and we'll do the rest."

"Agreed," Nathaniel responded as he shook the Roman's hand.

"Help me ... help me turn it over." Nathaniel felt sick and his head felt as if he was being stoned when he spoke. The other men grabbed the cross, heaved it up, and let it fall over.

A deep thud rang out as the cross hit the ground. Nathaniel closed his eyes and waited for the dust to clear. Sera saw it first and covered her face. She cried, "No. Oh, Lord ... no."

Several of the disciples recognized it and took a step back, realizing what had happened. Nathaniel slowly looked up through the dust. He had a mixture of dry and fresh blood and dirt on his cheeks. Tears ran down his face. The moment the cross came into focus, he began to heave and choke and turned away to throw up.

"My God, forgive me. What have I done?" he cried out, lying facedown in the dirt. Nathaniel's carpentry mark was on the base of the cross.

They all sat there for what seemed like an eternity. When the initial shock wore off, Peter said softly to the disciples, "Come on. It doesn't matter. Let's show them. Nathaniel, come. Get up. We have to show you something." The men helped Nathaniel and Sera to their feet and began to walk a short distance over to some tombs.

"No, I don't want to see," Nathaniel mumbled as Matthew and James supported him. "Why are you doing this? I don't want to see ..." he kept saying.

"Please, Nathaniel, please." Peter took James's place holding him up, and they let him down to the ground at the entrance of an empty tomb. He just sat there in a stupor, his head hanging toward the ground.

"Look inside," John said gently.

Nathaniel slowly raised his head and tried to focus on the dim interior of the tomb. He raised one hand to shield his eyes from the harsh sunlight. As his eyes adjusted, he began to make out a pile of crumpled graveclothes and a headcloth, a napkin folded very neatly where someone's head would lay. He was having trouble thinking and didn't understand why they were showing him any of this.

"Nathaniel ... he is risen. He's risen!" John said just loud enough for Sera to hear also. The disciples smiled, and Sera's tears turned to tears of joy. Nathaniel couldn't process what they were saying. "We've seen him. He told us he would rise ... remember?"

His thoughts were mixed up. He had taken for granted and dismissed much of what Jesus said out of confusion and disbelief. At that moment, he wished he hadn't. "Wait." Everyone looked at Nathaniel. He stared into the tomb at the napkin and remembered when Jesus turned water into wine in Cana.

"Nathaniel, what is it?" Peter asked.

"The napkin! The napkin!" Nathaniel laughed a little and winced in pain. He pointed into the tomb, and Andrew ran in and brought the napkin to him. He took it and ran his hand over the creases, over and over, smiling. "He said he would come back." He whispered, looking down at the napkin, "I didn't get it. It was right in front of me the whole time." Tears began to fall again as Nathaniel said the words. Sera came over and wrapped her arms around him. "He was with me every day." He looked at his wife.

"Peter, where is he?" Nathaniel wiped his face with his tunic and tried to collect himself.

"I don't know. We have seen him!" Peter said, trying to make sure Nathaniel understood.

Nathaniel slumped down, looking at the dirt. Remorse and regret filled him. "If I could just one time ..." He picked up a rock and tossed it into the open grave. He thought about their friendship and their adventures. He smiled when he thought about the vipers. He realized the truth he spoke when they tried to kill him in Nazareth.

"I can't believe this has happened." Nathaniel looked up at the disciples standing in front of him. He looked at Peter and began to quote Isaiah, shaking his head: "'He was despised and rejected by men, A man of sorrows and acquainted with grief. We hid *our* faces from him; he was despised, and we did not esteem him. Surely he has born our griefs and carried our sorrows; yet we thought of him as stricken, stricken by God, and afflicted'" (Isaiah 53:1–5 NKJV).

Suddenly, Sera gasped and jumped backward. The disciples were startled and stepped back, and then they began to smile.

Nathaniel sat frozen. From behind, someone placed two hands on Nathaniel's head, and his cuts were gone, and all his pain left his body. As he was healed, Nathaniel and the others heard him finish the scripture in Isaiah. "'But I *was* wounded for your transgressions, *I was* bruised for your iniquities; the chastisement

for your peace *was* upon me, and by my stripes you are healed'"
(Isaiah 53:1–5 NKJV).

Nathaniel spun around and burst into tears. "I'm sorry; I'm so sorry. Please forgive me."

Jesus smiled, looked at Sera, and motioned her over.

"Lord!" she cried out as they both held on to him and cried.

Jesus comforted them. "All is forgiven."

Through Nathaniel's tears, they could hear him say, "My Lord ... my God ... my friend."

And on that day, they believed.

Printed in the United States
By Bookmasters